Marc closed the doo.... ...., ..ood, not moving into the room, but looking at Jeni. And what she saw in his eyes made her heart pound, suffocatingly, in her throat.

'Jeni!' he breathed.

She was completely unprepared for this, completely vulnerable.

His arms were around her, drawing her to him. His mouth found hers and she opened her lips to the demand of his. She could feel his body, hard and strong against hers and she melted against him, knowing that she had been waiting for this all evening.

It was the memory of the children that won the battle for her. She had only the dimmest recollection of his wife, in the lounge at Heathrow, and he had said nothing to make her more flesh-and-blood to Jeni. But the children—she could visualise them vividly, could see them in their father's arms, kissing him goodbye.

She thrust her hands against his chest and forced her face back, away from his.

'Why did you have to do that?' she asked.

His face was pale now, and wiped clean of expression. He ran a hand through his hair and distractedly moved a few paces into the room.

'I'm sorry,' he said. 'I shouldn't have. . .it was too soon.'

'It will always be too soon,' she said. 'I'll never. . .'

For Judith Hunte, writing Medical Romances is a happy merging of two major interests, nursing and writing. Judith worked for several years as a librarian before beginning nursing training, eventually qualifying as a registered nurse and midwife. She left nursing to marry and have her family, a son and two daughters, then returned to work in various Australian hospitals for several years.

Early retirement has given her the opportunity to indulge a lifelong yen to write. Her own nursing experience provides the background for her stories.

Previous Titles

ENTER DR JONES
THE HEALING OF DR TRAVIS

LOVE AND DR ADAMS

BY

JUDITH HUNTE

MILLS & BOON LIMITED
ETON HOUSE   18–24 PARADISE ROAD
RICHMOND   SURREY   TW9 1SR

First published in Great Britain 1991
by Mills & Boon Limited

© Judith Hunte 1991

Australian copyright 1991
Philippine copyright 1991
This edition 1991

ISBN 0 263 77249 7

Set in 10 on 11½ pt Linotron Times
03-9105-54835
Typeset in Great Britain by Centracet, Cambridge
Made and printed in Great Britain

CHAPTER ONE

'QANTAS flight 401 for Sydney is now boarding at Gate Three.'

In the departure lounge of Heathrow Airport, two backs bent simultaneously. Two hands grasped the strap of a dark blue cabin bag. Two voices spoke in unison.

'Excuse *me*!'

'*Mine*, I think!'

Jeni Tremaine raised her head and looked into a pair of blue eyes only inches from hers. Marcus Adams saw a delicately featured face, framed in honey-blonde, softly waving shoulder-length hair, and large grey-blue eyes, alight with determination.

The impasse lasted about three seconds—just long enough for Jeni to realise that, although the bag she was clutching certainly looked like hers, the luggage tag dangling from its handle was unfamiliar. She released her hold and, as she straightened up, saw another, identical bag lying on the floor near where she had been sitting.

'I'm so sorry!' she said in confusion, gesturing towards the other bag. 'You can see why. . .they're so alike. . .'

The man interrupted her curtly. 'Of course. Think no more about it,' he said, and turned abruptly and walked away.

Although his words had been reassuring enough, there was something in his manner that left Jeni feeling slightly foolish, and more than a little resentful that he had not given her a chance to apologise more fully.

There was something vaguely familiar about him. It took her only a few moments to realise that she had seen him earlier, saying goodbye to his family, within a few feet of where she had been standing with her brother Philip. Jeni had kissed Philip, said a last farewell and moved through the security checkpoint, but the little family group remained, like a cameo, impressed on her mind. There was something idyllic about it. The man had one arm around a girl of about ten years who was standing on tiptoe to kiss him. His other hand rested on the shoulder of a boy somewhat younger. A woman, clearly the children's mother, stood watching, a small smile on her lips, waiting for her own farewell embrace.

Perhaps the so-recent parting from his family had been the reason for the man's curtness. Jeni put the incident from her mind, and moved to join the queue of passengers forming at the gate.

The plane was a wide-bodied jet and she had been allocated a window seat. There was no stewardess nearby, so, with some difficulty, she stowed her own cabin bag in the locker above her head, reflecting, not for the first time, that overhead lockers had not been designed with five-foot-four-inch females in mind.

She sat down, leaned her head back and breathed a small, silent prayer for a smooth flight. She was looking around her, approvingly, at the blue and grey décor of the cabin, with deep French blue carpet and lighter herringbone tweed seat covers, when she saw the man with the cabin bag like hers enter the plane and move slowly up the aisle, scanning seat numbers above the windows as he came.

Not wishing to be caught watching him, she dropped

her eyes and leaned forward to take a magazine from the pocket of the seat in front of her. A few moments later she became aware that he had paused at the row of three seats in which she was seated. Glancing up quickly, she saw him pocketing his ticket. Then, with a crisp economy of movement which appealed to the nurse in Jeni, he placed a black attaché case and a folded newspaper on the aisle seat, disposed of his cabin bag in a locker, picked up the paper and the attaché case, and sat down.

He nodded in her direction and said, 'Good morning,' but Jeni was sure he had not seen her, and certainly not recognised her. Everything about him— his reserved manner, his well-cut dark charcoal suit, the copy of *The Times* he was unfolding, was so typically English that she had to resist a mischievous impulse to reply, 'G'day, mate!'

Instead she murmured, 'Hello,', which he probably did not hear, and became as apparently absorbed in her magazine as he was in his paper. She hoped he got the message that she had no intention of attempting to breach his wall of reserve, or to annoy him with idle chatter.

Nobody came to claim the empty seat between them before the doors were shut and the plane began backing away from the terminal building. Jeni decided she had better resign herself to a long, quiet, tedious journey.

Not that that bothered her. After three months of living in a cramped London flat with a convalescent sister-in-law undergoing the rigours of chemotherapy treatment, a three-year-old nephew and an enchanting but demanding nine-month-old niece who had to be fed, changed, bathed, amused and bedded from morning to night, she could use a few hours of peace and quiet herself.

As she watched the stewardess miming the safety procedures with a reassuringly bored expression, Jeni recalled the night of Pip's urgent ISD call to Sydney. Sally had just had surgery for a lump in her breast. The lump had proved to be malignant and would need lengthy follow-up treatment. With two small children and a newly set-up business, Pip was having trouble coping. Could Jeni possibly help?

Jeni had just completed a year as staff nurse at her training hospital and was beginning a four-week break before taking up an appointment as sister at a private hospital on Sydney's lower north shore. The authorities had agreed to extend the one-month break to three, and she had left almost immediately for London.

Now she was returning, mission accomplished, and leaving behind her a sister-in-law whose prognosis was excellent, and a much relieved brother.

She had one week up her sleeve before she had to report for duty at her new job. She planned to spend most of that week soaking up the sun on the beach, wearing as little as possible, or messing about in the boat on the Harbour. A taste of an English winter, including a white Christmas, just passed, had been interesting and, in a centrally-heated apartment, she had not felt the cold too much. But there was nothing— just nothing—to compare with an Aussie summer. Her bones felt warmer at the mere thought of it.

The plane began to gather speed down the runway and, as it lifted off, Jeni leaned forward against the pull of gravity to catch a last glimpse of England. It was a cold morning, but the sun had broken through the clouds. Below them sprawled the buildings and runways of Heathrow. The plane banked, affording a brief glimpse of Windsor Castle. Jeni was able to make out a tiny flag fluttering from a turret, announcing that the

Queen was in residence. Then there were expanses of rapidly receding rooftops and a distant stretch of coastline, before they ran into a dense bank of white cloud.

The captain's voice over the intercom welcomed them aboard and gave details of their flight. Jeni replaced the magazine and took a paperback novel from her handbag. The man two seats away was extracting documents from his attaché case. With the decisiveness which seemed to characterise his movements, he drew a silver pen from his pocket, unscrewed the top of it and began making notes on the pages before him. He was completely absorbed in what he was doing. Jeni tried to concentrate on her book, but found her thoughts swinging between Pip and Sally back in London and Australia and home ahead.

After a while, a drinks trolley moved up the aisle. Jeni shook her head. The man next to her ordered a gin and tonic and, as it was handed to him, he closed the file he had been working on and placed it on the seat between them. By turning her head slightly and reading upside down, Jeni was able to make out its title—*The Diagnosis and Treatment of Raynaud's Phenomenon.*

Her interest in the man quickened. He was a doctor! Nobody else would be reading a paper like that, let alone be so absorbed in it. Understanding, as she did, the pressures of a doctor's life, the busy schedules, the demands on his time, the need to keep up with developments within his profession, she exonerated him completely for his unsociableness. He had probably been putting medical journals on one side for weeks before this flight, promising himself that he would read them on the plane. Perhaps later, when he had caught up on his reading, he would be more friendly.

She did not have to wait that long. Holding his drink carefully, he turned towards her with a polite smile, which immediately changed to a look of surprise.

'Hello again!' he said. 'Our paths seem fated to cross today.'

His smile made crinkly lines around his eyes and transformed his somewhat severe expression. His eyes were even bluer than she remembered. He had a strong, somewhat square-jawed face, with a firm mouth and straight black eyebrows beneath dark, crisply waving hair. He was handsome—definitely what her nursing friend Charlene would call a 'spunk'. Charlene was blonde and curvaceous and could no more help coming on to an attractive man than she could help breathing. Jeni did not succumb so readily, and anyway, good looks and charming smile aside, this man was married. That qualified him, in Jeni's book, to be nothing more than a congenial companion on a long flight. And she had a feeling that, if she were more than just politely friendly, he would retreat again behind that wall of reserve and not even be that.

She smiled back at him. 'I felt rather embarrassed about that. I hope you didn't think I was trying to purloin your bag.'

'Not at all. And if you had, you wouldn't have found anything of value or interest in it.'

Jeni was not too sure about that. Now was an opportunity to tell him that she was a nurse and just possibly might have more interest in his reading matter than he realised. But something held her back, perhaps that same instinct not to say anything that would make him think she was being too forthcoming, as claiming a common profession might possibly do.

'Are you going right through to Sydney?' he asked.

'Yes—I live there. And you?'

'I'm having a two-day stopover in Singapore before going on to Sydney.'

His voice was deep and resonant, his accent impeccably English.

She said, 'I had hoped to have a Singapore stopover, too, but I've left myself too little time.'

If he asked why she had to hurry back, she would tell him that she was a nurse. Instead he said, 'If I may say so, you don't sound Australian.'

She felt a flash of annoyance that he should categorise her by her speech. Then she realised that she had been guilty of just that, earlier, when she had pigeonholed him as 'typically English'.

She relaxed, then laughed and said, 'You mean because I don't sound like a female version of Paul Hogan?'

He gave a wry smile and said, 'I suppose I did have something like that in mind. I apologise.'

'Have you been to Australia before?' she asked.

'No. I have a close friend who lives in Sydney and who's finally talked me into coming.'

'I hope you won't be disappointed.'

'I should introduce myself. Marcus Adams.' He leaned across and held out his hand. His handshake was cool and firm.

'And I'm Jeni Tremaine.'

A stewardess with dinner menus prevented further conversation. Jeni ordered cold poached salmon with a Wyndham Estate Chardonnay, and a vanilla bavarois with cherries for dessert. Marcus Adams asked for fillet steak and a small bottle of claret.

Then, to Jeni's disappoin'ment, he returned to his reading. But she noticed that he was not so absorbed this time and, before long, that he wasn't reading at all but appeared lost in thought. Whatever he was thinking about was not making him happy. In fact, she sensed all at once, he was a man with a great deal on his mind.

When their meal came, he was still preoccupied and ate in silence, apart from one appreciative comment about the food, which really was excellent. Jeni's salad was temptingly served on a bed of red and green mignonette, with a julienne of fresh vegetables, surprisingly crisp for plane fare. Her dessert was light and tempting.

When the aisle was clear of food trolleys again, she moved around the plane for a while, stopping to chat with a friendly hostess who commented on the bright Ken Done scarf Jeni was wearing with her cream fine-knit pullover and taupe and cream checked pleated skirt. Then a woman somewhat older than herself, who was sitting alone, smiled at her, and she sat down beside her and chatted for a while.

When she returned to her own seat, Marcus Adams was still reading, but looked up with a quick smile as she moved past him.

Night came on quickly. She refused a headset for the movie which, predictably, was *Crocodile Dundee*, and which she had seen before. The night would be short since they were jetting eastwards, so she laid back her seat and settled down to get what sleep she could.

She had no idea how long she had been in a drowsy state, somewhere between sleeping and waking, when the PA system crackled and the captain's voice said, 'We are approaching an area of possible turbulence. This should last only a minute or two. Please extinguish all cigarettes and fasten your seatbelts.'

People stirred sleepily and stewardesses began moving along the aisles, checking seatbelts and speaking reassuringly to any passengers who appeared anxious.

Jeni turned her face towards the window so the hostess would not notice her state of panic. Her heart was thumping uncomfortably in her throat and there was a buzzing noise in her ears. She knew the symptoms only too well. She was not phobic about air travel, as long as it was smooth. But turbulence and air pockets, anything that sent the plane dropping through space, brought on an irrational, uncontrollable, primitive fear of falling.

She managed, despite her shaking fingers, to fasten her seatbelt, hoping that no one, especially Marcus Adams, would notice her panic. She tried to distract herself by watching the movie, but even the snapping jaws of a mechanical crocodile could not compete with her fear of what the next few minutes might bring.

A minute or two later the plane slipped sickeningly sideways as it hit the first of the turbulence. It steadied, then plummeted downwards. There was a general gasp throughout the plane, but Jeni did not hear it. She was isolated in her own world of terror. Her hands were clasped tightly in her lap, her teeth were clenched and her eyes were closed.

The downward plunge of the plane ceased abruptly, then, for what seemed an eternity, it became the plaything of the elements, slipping, sliding, bouncing.

A hand touched Jeni's arm, and a voice asked quietly, 'Are you all right?'

She turned a white face to Marcus Adams, who had slipped, unnoticed by her, into the seat next to her, and tried to smile at him through rigid lips. She began to say, 'Yes, thank you,' but the concern she saw in his eyes disarmed her and she mutely shook her head.

'Hold on to me,' he said.

He took her hand firmly in both of his and began talking quietly, matter-of-factly. He did not try to take her mind off her fears, but rather seemed to be encouraging her to face them and talk about them.

'You've experienced this before?' he asked.

'For as long as I can remember,' she replied shakily.

'Only in planes?'

'No. Mostly in planes. . .but in lifts too. . .the fast ones, in tall buildings.'

'Do you know what started it?' he asked.

'I can remember, as a small child, I hated being on a swing. . . Oh!' She caught her breath as the plane dropped suddenly again.

'Just breathe normally. In and out. . .in and out. . . That's better.'

And it was better. Even though the plane continued to plunge and toss intermittently and she was barely conscious of what he was saying, just the sound of his voice was reassuring. In a few minutes she felt able to speak again.

'You're very kind. I'm sorry to be a nuisance.'

'No, not at all. It's a fairly common phobia.' He sounded as though he was called on to quieten panic-stricken passengers every day of the week. 'At least you haven't let it stop you flying,' he continued.

'Not yet, anyway,' she replied with a tremulous smile. 'I'd despise myself if I did that. And I'm too keen on travelling to let it ground me.'

'It would certainly be limiting if you had to go everywhere by sea—Australia being an island.'

The plane had been stable for several minutes, but he still held her hand, and she found it extraordinarily comforting. Eventually, she gave a small sigh and drew her hand away, trying to sound casual as she said, 'Thank you, Doctor. I think your patient will live.'

He raised a quizzical eyebrow. 'Is it as obvious as all that that I'm a doctor?' he asked.

'I happened to see the title of the paper you were reading earlier. I couldn't imagine anyone but a doctor being so absorbed in a subject like that.'

'I guess not.'

She hoped that her reference to his reading material would not make him suspect that she was a nurse, because, at the moment, she felt anything but a credit to her training. Fortunately, he seemed equally chary about discussing *his* profession. He changed the subject abruptly, saying, 'Perhaps you'll be able to get some sleep now.'

'I'm sure I shall. And thank you again.'

He gave her a long, clinical look, then nodded, as if satisfied, touched her hand briefly, and returned to his own seat.

There was movement and a murmur of voices through the plane as passengers, relieved that it was all over, unfastened their seatbelts, adjusted their seats and settled down again. Nobody appeared to have noticed Jeni's panic, and that was entirely due to the unobtrusive way in which her companion had intervened and helped her through her bad moments.

From there on the flight was uneventful. They had a brief refuelling stop at Bombay and eventually dropped down into Singapore's busy Changi Airport. They were told they would have an hour and a half before their flight resumed.

Marcus Adams turned to Jeni.

'Are you going through to the terminal?' he asked.

'I'm still a little shaky,' she admitted. 'I might just sit in the transit lounge and watch the world go by.'

'I think some exercise would do you good. I'd be happy to wander round the shops with you for a while.'

'Oh, no!' Jeni protested. 'I can't impose on you any more. And don't you have someone meeting you?'

'No, my time's my own while I'm here. The invitation stands.'

Suspecting that he could become impatient if she dithered any longer, she said, 'Then, thank you, I accept.'

Once in the hustle and bustle of the duty-free shopping area, she realised that she was, indeed, still weak in the legs. Marcus Adams, sensing this, took her hand in his and guided her through the throng of travellers pushing and shoving, all intent on making the best possible purchase in the limited time available.

Jeni could not decide whether his attitude towards her was paternal or professional. A little of each, perhaps. In either case, she enjoyed the sense of security it gave her. She glanced up at him, wondering how old he was. With a child of around ten, he could hardly be less than thirty-five, though he did not look that old.

Aware of her gaze, he looked down at her and raised his eyebrows, curious as to what had been going through her mind. She could not tell him, so she just smiled and turned to examine a shop window. They browsed contentedly in and out of shops. Jeni was completely at ease and sensed that he felt the same.

He made sure they had plenty of time for the walk back to the departure gate. At the gate, Jeni said, 'Goodbye,' and held out her hand. He said softly, 'Goodbye, Jeni,' then bent swiftly and kissed her cheek. Surprised, she smiled at him mistily, before he turned and walked quickly away.

Feeling as though she had lost a friend, she watched his tall figure disappear into the crowd. As she walked down the airbridge and on to the plane, she could almost still feel his hand holding hers. Certainly she could feel the place on her cheek where he had kissed

her. She raised a hand and touched the spot. Back in
her seat, she stared out of the window, watching the
activity on the tarmac below and trying to still a strange
agitation within her. She chided herself for reacting so
strongly to a casual encounter with a man she would
never see again. But, as the minutes passed before
take-off, she became more and more conscious of the
empty seats beside her.

In the air again, she managed to doze for a time.
When she woke she saw that they were flying high
above the hazy contours of what must be northern
Australia. The plane seemed motionless, poised in
space. But she knew that it was eating up the miles
between herself and home. She would soon be landing
in Sydney.

And Tony would be there to meet her.

She had planned to return to Australia with answers
to questions that Tony had been asking her for some
time—and that she had been asking herself. With half
a world separating her from him, and with all the
busyness of her time in London, it had been easy to
procrastinate, to leave the problem of herself and Tony
in the too-hard-to-handle basket. But she couldn't
leave it there much longer.

Tony Carter was a doctor, now halfway through a
residency in the Sydney hospital where Jeni had trained
as a nurse. They had drifted together about nine
months ago, during her last year of training.

Using the months of intensive study that lay ahead
of her as an excuse, she had resisted Tony's growing
pressure to become more involved—in fact, to live
together, at least as often as their duty rosters allowed.

Jeni had a flat in Manly. It was a beach holiday flat
which her family had owned for years and which she
had taken over during her first year of training and for

which she insisted on paying her parents a nominal
rental. Overlooking a wide expanse of Pacific Ocean,
it had been an ideal bolt-hole when she had felt the
need to get away from the pressure of hospital life or
when she had to find a quiet place to study on days off.

She reserved the main bedroom of the flat for
herself. The other bedroom was available for any of
her crowd at the hospital who likewise needed a refuge
from time to time. There was a tacit understanding that
those who used the flat leave something in the jar for
running expenses, and that they contribute their fair
share to the larder. Three of her friends—Tony, Liz
and Charlene—had been given keys to the flat before
she went overseas. Tony had left her in no doubt that
he hoped to be granted permanent residential rights on
her return.

Tony was a nice guy and they had much in common.
It was their mutual love of the surf and the sea which
had first brought them together. As a teenager, Tony
had made a name for himself as a 'surfie', and could
possibly have become a professional surfer if he had
not chosen to go into medicine. He had almost white,
sun-bleached hair and a fair complexion which,
although deeply tanned, still retained a tendency to
sunburn if his hospital duties kept him indoors for too
many days at a stretch. He was intelligent rather than
intellectual, happy-go-lucky about everything except
his profession, and generous to a fault.

A great-uncle had left him a surprise legacy which
he had promptly spent on a boat, and he was now as
enthusiastic a sailor as he had been a board-rider. Jeni
suspected that his boat was the true love of his life.

With the same prodigality with which he had spent
his windfall on a boat instead of putting it aside to buy
a medical practice later on, he had made the boat

available to his friends. They were mostly young medicos too, all about as impecunious as one another, but they dobbed in to pay for mooring the boat in a sheltered bay at Clontarf in Sydney's Middle Harbour, and for its yearly week in the slips for essential maintenance.

Under his tuition, Jeni had become a proficient sailor, and whenever their off-duty times coincided she and Tony would be on the boat, pottering about doing odd jobs, or sailing on the Harbour.

Tony's friendship, hectic days at work, halcyon days on the Harbour, social outings with their wide, easygoing circle of friends—it all added up to a lifestyle which was very much to Jeni's liking.

Yet today, when she was returning home, with the prospect of meeting her friends and Tony again, and with the challenge of a new job ahead of her, she was acutely aware, for the first time in her life, of an emptiness—a sort of dissatisfaction—deep within herself. Would living with Tony, marrying him, perhaps, fill that void in her?

Purposefully, Jeni tried to visualise what life with Tony would be like. She drew mental pictures of them together in the flat. . .waking up with him beside her in the morning. . .coming home to him after work. . . The pictures were clear enough. But her senses didn't respond. Her pulse didn't quicken.

In a moment of clarity she saw that more conclusive than all her weighings of pros and cons would be her reaction when she saw Tony in a few minutes' time. Her feelings then would surely give her the answer she sought.

Almost imperceptibly, the plane was losing height. She usually dreaded landing, but today it did not seem to bother her. It was almost as though Marcus Adams was still there beside her. She remembered every word he had said to her as he sat holding her hand, the quiet reassurance of his voice, his steady, concerned gaze. It seemed so real she almost felt that if she reached out she could touch him. She did indeed raise her arm, then, feeling slightly silly, let it fall on the arm-rest beside her. It would have been nice if he had not stopped off at Singapore. They had just begun to get to know one another. Those few extra hours. . . She would have enjoyed sharing his first sight of Sydney—pointing out to him the Harbour, the city buildings, the Bridge, the Opera House.

Soon they were making a wide, slow turn over the broad expanse of water that was Botany Bay, and levelling out for the approach to the runway at Mascot Airport. The runway jutted far out into the Bay, and Jeni felt sure, for one panicky moment, that they were coming down in the water.

Her progress through Customs was slow, but eventually she was pushing her luggage-laden trolley out into the Arrivals lounge and past the press of faces on the other side of the barrier. Tony had obviously seen her before she picked him out in the crowd. He was smiling and waving and, in the few moments it took for her to clear the barrier and wait for him to push his way to her through the crowd, she was able to identify her feeling on seeing him again as being no more than a warm, friendly glow.

They hugged and kissed briefly, more like friends than lovers. Jeni was relieved about that, because it indicated that Tony was not about to demand instant answers from her about their future.

Nevertheless, it *was* good to be home. She sighed with contentment as they walked briefly out into warm sunshine on their way to the car park. Tony turned his head and smiled at her. 'Good to be back?' he asked.

She nodded happily. 'Do you have the whole day off?' she asked.

'Just the morning, I'm afraid.'

She settled down in Tony's red Honda for the drive into the city and beyond to Manly.

'How's the gang?' she asked. 'Have you seen much of Liz and Charlene while I've been away?'

Tony seemed to be pondering his reply, but eventually he said, 'Liz was transferred to Men's Medical soon after you left, so we've seen a fair bit of each other about the ward. Charlene is still in ENT.'

'And hating it as much as ever, I suppose! Poor Charlene—those eternal tonsils and adenoids.' Then, with a sudden burst of nostalgia, she said, 'You know, I think I could even put up with Ts and As all day if it meant being back with you all. I don't know why I ever wanted to leave.'

Tony did not reply, seeming intent on his driving. After a while, he said, 'I've got a very busy week ahead of me, Sunshine. I don't know whether I'll be able to see you again before you start work.'

Jeni was disappointed, even though she understood. It was not unusual for Tony's ward work to tie him up for days at a stretch.

'Not to worry,' she said. 'I plan to laze about on the beach most days and get my tan back. And Mother and Dad will be down for a couple of days soon.'

'Good. Say "hi" to them for me.'

'Will do. If you happen to have a chance to take the boat out, you will let me know?'

'Of course. But I don't think it likely.'

He turned his head and their eyes held for a moment. As he looked back at the road, his left hand left the steering-wheel and closed over hers, which was lying in her lap. He squeezed it firmly and said, 'We really have missed you, hon. And you're looking great. Don't ruin that lovely English complexion with too much sun all at once, will you?'

They were on the Cahill expressway now, approaching the Bridge. Jeni, looking down at Circular Quay with its medley of water craft coming and going, knew for a certainty that this was where she belonged and that she was glad to be back.

Crossing the Spit Bridge, en route to Manly, she leaned forward to peer down to the right.

Tony grinned. 'Yes! She's still there!'

'Have you done much to her since I left?'

'I finally replaced those jib sheets. And I managed to drop another winch handle overboard.'

Jeni laughed. 'Now I don't feel so guilty about dropping the first one,' she said, then added, 'Will you have time for a cup of coffee?'

'Just a quick one.'

Most of the windows of Jeni's flat, which was on the top floor of a big old house on the beachfront, looked out across the ocean. They drank their coffee, sitting at the table in the window of the living-room. Just the width of the road and a strip of lawn separated them from white sand and curling breakers. Beyond was blue-green water as far as the eye could see. Even mid-morning on a Monday, there were surfers in the water, taking advantage of a three-metre swell.

Very soon Tony said goodbye, with another quick hug and a kiss. It was with an odd mixture of disappointment and relief that Jeni listened to his footsteps fade away down the passage.

CHAPTER TWO

THE NEXT week passed much as Jeni anticipated. She spent a lot of time on the telephone, catching up with friends. She walked, she swam, she lay on the beach when the sun was not too fierce. Her parents came to Sydney, but could spend only one night with her because of the seasonal demands of their property in Parkes, about two hundred miles inland from Sydney.

Tony rang once, Liz not at all. Charlene phoned and met her for a morning's shopping in the city.

By Monday morning Jeni was more than ready to don uniform and report for duty at the private hospital in Cremorne, which had been holding her appointment in abeyance for three months.

Nursing in this hospital would be very different from that which she had known previously. But that was what she wanted—to broaden her experience with a different kind of nursing.

Two beautiful old double-storeyed colonial homes, with tall white pillars and lots of white iron lace, had been joined by a long, triple-storeyed, unobtrusively modern wing, to form the hospital. Men's and women's medical and surgical wards occupied the original buildings. Everything else—operating suites, radiology, laboratories, central supply, day-care wards, reception areas—was located in the middle wing.

The hospital was high on a hill, overlooking the Harbour. Several magnificent old trees had been retained and gardens landscaped around them. The gardens were used mainly by ambulant patients and those who could be taken outside in wheelchairs.

Because the everyday comings and goings of the hospital were through the rear, where the buildings faced on to a busy street, the gardens remained quiet and secluded, with glimpses of water between the trees.

On the day before her interview with Matron, now almost four months ago, Jeni had gone to the hospital during visiting hours to 'case the joint', as she told Charlene. She had walked along corridors, trying to look as though she knew where she was going. She had peeped into a vacant two-bed room whose door stood ajar. She opened a door marked 'Treatment-Room' and had time to register that it was well-equipped and shining, before feigning surprise and muttering, 'Sorry—wrong room,' to two nurses perched on stools, drying trays of instruments.

Everywhere was a degree of opulence she had never encountered in a hospital before. She thought hard and long about the difference that was likely to make to nursing standards, before deciding that, if the hospital offered her a position, she would accept it.

Now she was about to get answers to the questions she had asked herself.

Helen McMahon, sister in charge of Women's Surgical, where Jeni had been told to report, was tall and pencil-slim, with dark blue eyes and black hair smoothly upswept under her dainty starched cap. Large square blue-rimmed glasses added to her sophisticated appearance. But she seemed friendly, as she and Jeni sat talking, after the night sister had finished reading her report and the three day nurses had gone about their duties.

'I can't believe this is a duty-room,' Jeni said, looking around her in amazement.

Helen laughed. 'I know what you mean. You'll get used to it.'

There was carpet on the floor—dark grey to blend with silver-grey walls. On one wall was a large modern print, framed in black. The table was black-topped and shiny, and the chairs were contoured and upholstered in a blue-grey material. The only indications that this was, in fact, a duty-room were a trolley of case-notes against one wall and several lists of treatments and medications, encased in clear plastic, on the table. A sphygmomanometer also lay on the table, but Helen picked it up and popped it into a drawer. There was a complete absence of the clutter which Jeni had always associated with duty-rooms. Capes, cardigans, hand-bags, umbrellas were kept in lockers in the staff-room next door, where there were changing facilities and enough mirrors to ensure that the staff went on duty with their make-up intact and not a hair out of place.

Helen said, 'I'll be busy with doctors' rounds for an hour or so. I wonder what you can do until I'm free to show you around.'

'I'm quite happy to read the report again and browse through case-notes,' Jeni assured her.

Helen thought for a moment. 'We have a patient for surgery at eight-thirty, a Mrs Jackson. She's to have a partial gastrectomy for a deep gastric ulcer and is very apprehensive—probably cancerophobic, in fact. I think I'll take you along and introduce you to her. Then you can stay with her—go with her to OR if you think that will reassure her.'

'Fine! Are they sure she hasn't got cancer?'

Helen stood up and selected a file from the case-note trolley.

'She's had gastroscopy and a biopsy. Here's a photo of the ulcer, taken endoscopically.'

Jeni studied the small, shiny coloured photograph attached to the file.

'It does look nasty. She's lucky not to have perforated. It's probably the pain she's been having that's convinced her she has cancer.'

'She's a chronic worrier—a typical ulcer type. Come along, then, and I'll introduce you to her. Her pre-op preparation has been done, as you heard in the report, and her pre-med injection is due about now.'

As they walked out of the room, they met a nurse about to enter it, carrying a small kidney dish in which were two small glass phials which she held up for Helen to see.

'Morphine 0.6 and Atrophine 100 mgs,' said Helen. 'Give it right away, nurse. Here are the case-notes, so you can chart it. Sister Tremaine and I are just going along to see Mrs Jackson.'

As they walked along the corridor, Helen explained, 'Mrs Jackson has been in one of our pre-op units for a couple of days, resting before her surgery.'

She knocked on a door and they entered what looked to Jeni more like a luxury motel unit than a hospital room. It was decorated in soft pastel tonings and, besides the bedroom area, had a lounge area with two deep armchairs, a coffee-table or two, a small refrigerator and a television set. French doors opened on to a balcony which overlooked the Harbour. Jeni was to find that as many of the patients' rooms as possible had this view, with facilities such as treatment-rooms, storage closets, utility-rooms being at the rear of the buildings.

A small, thin woman, in about her middle forties, lay in the bed, the green theatre cap covering her hair looking incongruous against the pretty pink floral bedspread. Helen greeted her cheerily, patting her hand, then holding it for a moment, to check her pulse.

'That's fine. Nurse's injection will make you nice and relaxed and without a care in the world. This is Sister Tremaine—Jeni. She's going to stay with you now and go with you to the theatre. You remember you'll be in a different room then.'

Helen, like a good nurse should, was projecting her patient's thoughts beyond the operation, making the assumption for her that all would be well.

When Helen had gone, Jeni chatted with Mrs Jackson for a while, but, seeing her become drowsy, she sat down in one of the armchairs and studied the case-note file. By the time the OR trolley arrived, she had registered most of its contents.

The OR suites were on the top floor of the middle wing of the hospital. As their little procession moved along a corridor towards OR, Jeni caught a glimpse, through a wide window, of a panorama of Sydney Harbour. The morning sun was turning the water to sparkling silver. There was a bustle of traffic on the water, and in the second or two it took to pass the window she saw a hydrofoil ferry come into view, trailing its white wake. It would be crowded with passengers, city-bound from Manly. Outside, life went on as usual. Here in OR attention was centred exclusively on the patient, now being transferred from trolley to table.

Jeni did not enter the operating-room itself with the trolley, but stopped in an ante-room to slip into a long white gown, put on a floral disposable theatre cap which completely covered her hair, and to tie on a mask. Then she went on into the theatre.

OR Sister, wearing a green gown, was standing behind her instrument table, the cover of which had been removed, checking its contents. Jeni introduced herself to her, explaining why she was there and asking permission to remain until Mrs Jackson was anaesthetised. She moved across to speak to Mrs Jackson, squeezed her shoulder reassuringly, then took up a position against a wall where Mrs Jackson could see her, but where she would be out of the way of the surgical team. She could hear the swish of brushes and the running of water in the scrub-room next door, and the murmur of male voices, but could not make out what they were saying.

The anaesthetist entered.

'Hello,' he said cheerily to the patient on the table. 'Remember me? I'm the chap who listened to your chest last night. Now, if I can have your arm for a minute. Fine!' He swabbed the injection site with alcohol. 'Just a tiny prick, that's all.'

Almost before he had laid aside the syringe and picked up an endotracheal tube, Mrs Jackson was asleep, breathing deeply and evenly.

Jeni could have left now, but, knowing she was not really needed on the ward, she decided to stay and observe for a few minutes longer.

Two doctors, in complete theatre garb which covered all but their eyes, had been standing together, with their gloved hands raised. Now they moved into place, one on either side of the table, the surgeon facing towards Jeni, his assistant with his back to her. A cover was removed from Mrs Jackson's abdomen, the assistant surgeon wielded long, swab-holding forceps to apply antiseptic lotion to the area in widening circular sweeps, then green drapes were dropped into place, leaving only the incision site exposed.

The surgeon held out his hand, the instrument nurse slapped a scalpel into it and he made the first incision.

His movements were confident and precise. That was

to be expected of any surgeon. But there was something about his hands, in the pale cream-coloured surgical gloves, which caused Jeni to hold her breath and look more closely at the man bent over the table.

As though he sensed her watching him, he looked up and their eyes met for a second. The fleeting glance was enough for her to be sure that it really was Marcus Adams there on the other side of the OR table. He had looked down again before she had time to see whether there had been any recognition in his eyes.

The operation continued smoothly and she had time to get her breath and begin to collect her thoughts. She had left Marcus Adams in Singapore, thinking never to see him again. In the days since then, she had thought about him more than she cared to admit to herself. And now here he was, just a few feet away from her, calmly operating and looking very much as though he belonged here. If that was so—if he was going to be working in the hospital as a surgeon, and she as a nurse. . . A tremor of excitement ran down her spine at the thought.

Fascinated, she watched him work, and listened to him talking with other members of the surgical team as he worked. Two things became clear: this was the first time he had operated in the hospital, and it would not be the last.

After a while he straightened his back and stretched, while the assisting surgeon clamped and tied a leaking blood vessel. He looked directly across at Jeni and this time his eyes lingered on her. They seemed puzzled, and she knew that he had not yet recognised her behind the effective disguise of her theatre attire.

'Nurse!' he said, looking directly at her. 'Would you retie the top string of my mask, please?'

He spoke crisply, as though he was used to instant

obedience from nursing staff. Jeni was in a quandary. To do as he asked, she would have to move right around the room, passing Sister's instrument tables as she went, and running the risk of contaminating one or other of the surgical team.

Sister turned her head and, by the merest flicker of an eye, indicated to Jeni that she remain where she was. Then she looked at the circulating nurse, who was standing behind Marcus Adams. Nurse promptly moved forward, retied the offending strings and stepped back. It was all done in seconds, using the almost telepathic ability that operating-room staff had to communicate with their eyes.

Nevertheless, Sister seemed to feel she should make some explanation to the surgeon.

'Sister came from the ward with the patient because she was feeling apprehensive about the surgery,' she told him.

'Are you still feeling apprehensive, Sister?' he asked, his glance flicking up to hold Jeni's momentarily.

Jeni did not reply. One of the nurses tittered. Sister OR raised her eyebrows expressively, as much as to say, So our new boy is a Smart Aleck! Aloud, she explained patiently, as if dealing with a not too bright child, 'It was Mrs Jackson who was feeling nervous, Doctor.'

'Oh?' One dark eyebrow shot up towards his cap. 'She seems to be quite relaxed at the moment.'

Again there was a quickly suppressed titter from the scout nurse.

Jeni was glad the mask hid the flush which had begun to creep into her cheeks. She made a move to leave the theatre, but his voice stopped her.

'Why was Mrs Jackson apprehensive? Didn't she sleep on her sedation?'

Jeni was thankful she had spent that time in Mrs Jackson's room earlier, studying her case-notes. She was able to reply, 'She had one hundred milligrams of Seconal at nine p.m. and she slept well.'

'Ah-*huh*!'

Jeni knew intuitively that the note of satisfaction in his voice was not because his patient had had a good night, but because he had, on hearing her voice for the first time, been able to place who she was. He looked up at her again and this time there was recognition, surprise and the hint of a smile in his eyes.

As soon as she could, Jeni excused herself to Sister and returned to the ward.

Helen McMahon was still occupied with a doctor doing a round, so Jeni sat down in the duty-room with the night report in front of her. But she found it hard to concentrate on the words on the page, her mind occupied with the extraordinary coincidence that she and Marcus Adams, when they met on the plane, had both been on their way to begin work in the same hospital, almost on the same day.

'Hello, you're back. How's the op going?' Helen's voice interrupted her thoughts.

'Fine, so far, although they hadn't reached the ulcer when I left.' Then she asked, although she already knew the answer, 'Who is the surgeon?'

'A Mr Adams. He's new—an Englishman who's bought into a surgical practice in the Clinic. They say he's very competent.'

'He seems to be. Will he be doing much work in the hospital?' asked Jeni.

'I expect so. Mrs Jackson in his first case here. It will depend on how quickly his practice builds up as to how much we see of him. I guess his partners will put patients his way for a while. They have a very busy practice. You do understand the set-up here?' Helen asked.

'Only vaguely.'

'Then let's talk over a cup of coffee.'

They went into the staff-room next door and helped themselves to coffee from the café bar. A tray bearing a plate of fresh scones and bowls of apricot jam and cream was on the table.

'We're allowed to have morning and afternoon tea in here,' Helen explained, 'but main meals have to be taken in the staff dining-room.'

They spread their scones with jam and cream and sat down. Helen launched into her explanation.

'The hospital is private, as you know. It's run by a board. There's a large clinic next door. That's owned by one of the medical partnerships occupying it—a firm of pathologists, actually. They lease suites to other medical practitioners. There's every kind of practice you could mention, including a twenty-four-hour general practice.'

'So the hospital and the clinic are separately owned?'

'Yes, but they're mutually beneficial. It's handy for the doctors to have a hospital on their doorstep and, in their turn, they keep our beds pretty well filled. Of course, the ultra-sophisticated stuff, like cranial and cardiac surgery, has to go to bigger hospitals like the Royal North Shore. But there's not much else we can't handle. We don't have a casualty unit—the patients are all admitted under the care of their own doctors. We still get our share of emergency surgery, but it comes through the doctors, not off the streets.'

'One gets the impression we cater to a wealthy clientèle?' queried Jeni.

'Not exclusively. But, because of our North Shore location, we do have a fair proportion of patients who are not dependent on health insurance to pay their hospital bills, but want the comforts, in hospital, to which they're accustomed at home.'

'It's a new kind of nursing to me.'

'I hope not.' Helen looked at her sharply. 'Rich people feel just as bad when they're sick as anyone else, and they're entitled to the same sort of nursing care. I've been here for two and a half years and I've never heard anyone suggest that we should make any distinction between patients in the private rooms and those in share and four-bed wards. Just nurse as you've always done—according to the needs of your patients—and forget about the size of their bank accounts.'

'I can't say how relieved I am to hear you say that. I did wonder, and worry a bit, about what difference it would make,' Jeni confessed.

Helen stood up and dropped her paper cup into a swing-top tidy. Jeni did likewise and followed her into the duty-room and waited while she sorted through a pile of letters which lay on the table.

'I'll take you round to meet the patients now,' said Helen. 'We might as well deliver these as we go.'

They did a leisurely round, stopping to chat with most of the patients to whom Helen introduced Jeni. It was that nice time of day in a hospital's routine when cleaning was finished, flowers freshly arranged, doctors' rounds completed and the patients relaxed. In the big day-room, several ladies were sitting, drinking tea and comparing notes on their doctors' visits. On a balcony, through French doors, several more, in white rattan easy chairs, were watching the scene on the Harbour.

'It's never the same for two minutes. I could sit here

watching it all day,' said one lady, whom Helen introduced as Anne Morrow. Anne was a schoolteacher,
Helen told Jeni. She looked to be in her late thirties
and, at first glance, seemed unattractive. But as she
talked her face became animated. She had a twinkle in
her eye, a quick intelligence and a dry sense of humour,
all of which instantly appealed to Jeni. Helen told Jeni
later that Anne also had a combination of compassion
and common sense that had, even in the week since
her kidney transplant, helped more than one other
patient in the unit to get their problems into
proportion.

As the two sisters finished their round and turned
into the corridor leading back to the duty-room, a tall
figure in a white starched coat was walking in the same
direction a little ahead of them. His head was high, his
arms relaxed and swinging, and he was whistling softly
to himself—a cheerful if not melodious tune.

'The picture of a satisfied surgeon,' murmured
Helen.

'Good,' said Jeni. She was happy that Mrs Jackson's
surgery appeared to have gone well. But she was more
interested, just at that moment, in her very imminent
meeting with Marcus Adams. In fact, she was feeling
quite unaccountably nervous about it. She realised that
the palms of her hands were damp.

Marcus Adams stopped at the door of the duty-
room, looked in and, seeing no one there, turned as
they approached him. His hair was still slightly flat-
tened from wearing the theatre cap, as though he had
not stopped to comb it. A stethoscope protruded from
the pocket of his coat.

He looked first at Helen, with a courteous, 'Good
morning, Sister', and then he turned to Jeni. There was
a lightening of his expression and the corners of his

mouth curved in a smile. Jeni's eyes twinkled back at him.

'Well. . .!' he said.

Helen interrupted. 'You haven't met our new sister, Doctor.'

'On the contrary, we have met.'

Helen looked surprised at first, then said, 'Of course! In OR.'

'Even before then,' he told her. 'We kept each other company on the plane from London a week ago.' He turned back to Jeni. 'How was the rest of your flight? Trouble-free, I hope?'

Jeni flushed slightly, knowing to what he was referring. She wished he could have forgotten about that.

'Yes, it was,' she said. 'And you? Did you enjoy your stopover in Singapore?'

'Actually, I rather wished I hadn't committed myself to that. I would have preferred, in the circumstances, to have come straight on to Sydney.'

Surely he could not mean. . .?

He looked at his watch with a quick flick of the wrist and said, 'I must go—I'm already late for my consulting session. By the way, Mrs Jackson is in Recovery. All was well. You should be seeing her soon. Call me if you need me, Sister.'

His brief smile encompassed them both and he was gone.

Helen pondered. 'Now why, if he was running late, did he bother to come to the ward? He told us nothing about Mrs Jackson we wouldn't have known anyway, from OR.'

Jeni thought she knew why.

'I think it may have been to find out whether it was really me he saw in OR. I was masked and gowned, of course. He strikes me as the kind of person who always has to have his facts in order, however trivial they might be.'

'But wasn't he expecting to find you here? Didn't you talk about it on the plane?'

'Oddly enough, we didn't. In fact, I didn't even tell him I was a nurse, and he didn't seem to want to talk about being a doctor.'

Helen raised her eyebrows, but before she could say any more a patient came up to ask whether she could change her dinner order. While Helen straightened that matter out, Jeni went into the duty-room, drew the trolley of case-notes alongside the table and sat down. She was not aware that there was a smile on her face until Helen came in and, looking at her shrewdly, asked, 'Do you always enjoy your work so much? Or is there some other reason why you look like the cat that's swallowed the cream? A reason like a tall, dark and handsome doctor?'

Jeni knew she had to nip in the bud the speculation she saw in Helen's face and said quickly, 'Please don't jump to conclusions. There's absolutely nothing like that—nor ever will be.'

'It's early days yet. Give it time,' said Helen.

'Time's not a factor, if it's Dr Adams we're talking about.'

'You disappoint me. It's about time we had a lovely staff romance. You're sure you can't oblige?'

'Definitely not! The man's married.'

'Really? Now I *am* disappointed. I was sure that was a romantic look I saw in his eye.'

'He's not only married,' Jeni added. 'He has two children.'

'Oh, well! That's that, then!'

That certainly should have been that! Jeni wished she could accept the inevitable as readily as Helen had done. Perhaps, as time went on and she became used to seeing Marcus Adams about the hospital, she would be able to accept him as just another doctor among the hundreds she had met, worked with and eventually all but forgotten about.

But she suspected that she had some way to go before she could aspire to that happy state of indifference.

CHAPTER THREE

JENI was in the duty-room next morning, charting medications, when Marcus Adams and an older man entered.

Marcus nodded and smiled at her, and continued his conversation, but he soon checked and said, 'I don't expect you've met Sister Tremaine, Bill.'

'Bill' seemed surprised that his new partner should be in a position to introduce a member of the staff to him. He looked at Jeni with an appreciative gleam in his eye, and said, 'No, I haven't had that pleasure.'

He was a tall, slightly portly man with iron-grey hair and a trim moustache. An old soldier, Jeni thought, and visualised him marching through the streets of Sydney on Anzac Day, with a group of comrades that dwindled in size year by year.

Marcus Adams said to her, 'This is my partner—one of them—Dr Bill Bennett. Sister Jeni Tremaine,' to Bill.

'How do you do?' Bill responded. 'Are you an old friend of Marc's?'

'Oh, no,' said Jeni hastily.

Marcus explained, 'Sister is as new to the hospital as I am. We met on the plane from London about a week ago.'

'You're English, too, then, Sister?'

'No, I'm very much an Aussie. I was returning home from visiting my family in London.'

Dr Bennett nodded, then turned back to resume his interrupted conversation. Jeni continued her charting.

'Sorry, Marc. You were saying. . .how old the children are.'

'Yes. Sarah's ten, I think, and Kim almost seven.'

'And you hope to find a school for them not too far from the hospital?'

'Not necessarily—though I do like what I've seen of the area.'

'Do you want a co-ed school?'

'It's what they've been used to. And it would make transport to and fro easier. Kim's been a trifle insecure, and the move from England won't help. I think he'd be happier at the same school as Sarah.'

Bill Bennett pondered, stroking his moustache. He shook his head.

'Really, you know, Marc, I'm not the best person to advise you about this. It's a good few years since I've had to worry about schools, and I'm afraid there'll have been a lot of changes since then. Perhaps Sister here. . .?' He turned to Jeni. 'Are you from Sydney, Sister?'

'My parents live in Parkes, but I started school down here when I was ten.'

'Which school?'

'Abbotsleigh.'

'An excellent school. I think you could be just the one to help Marc with his problem.' He turned to his partner. 'I'll leave you with Sister, Marc. I must finish my round. I've got that nephrectomy later and I must squeeze in a bite to eat some time too.'

He flicked a wrist to look at his watch, clicked his tongue and walked out.

Left alone, Jeni and Marc looked at each other in silence for a long moment, Jeni tentatively, Marc with a small, enigmatic smile. He shook his head, almost in disbelief, and said, 'It really is most extraordinary, finding you here like this.'

'Coincidence has a very long arm,' she agreed.

'Yes. I had thought we were just—er. . .'

'Ships that pass in the night?' Jeni supplied.

'Not quite appropriate, but something like that. Anyway, it certainly is nice to see you again.'

He made a slight movement of his hand, then checked swiftly, so she could not be sure what he had intended, except that she too had had an impulse to reach out and make physical contact with him—just a touch—to recapture, perhaps, those moments in the plane when he had held her hand and been so kind and understanding.

Suddenly there was an awareness between them, as if each knew what had been in the other's mind. But there was no awkwardness, no embarrassment—just a growing sense of affinity.

Belatedly, Jeni remembered that she must go and check up on the patient to whom she had given an injection a little while ago.

'How urgent is the decision about a school?' she asked.

'Fairly urgent.'

'I'll think about it overnight and talk to you tomorrow.' Her heart lifted at the thought that she would be seeing him again so soon.

'That would be good. Or. . .' He hesitated. 'Better still, are you free later today?'

'My shift finishes at three-thirty.'

'My own schedule is singularly undemanding at present,' he said. 'If you could spare the time to drive round with me and point out one or two possible schools, I could get some first impressions and narrow the field somewhat.'

'Sounds a good idea. Why don't I drive? My car's in the car park here, and I know my way around Sydney. It would leave you free to look around.'

'Great! I'll meet you outside the Clinic at, say, three forty-five?'

'Maybe I should warn you about my car,' said Jeni. 'It's not exactly the latest model. In fact, it's a beat-up little blue V-dub.'

'As long as it goes.'

'It does that—just.'

'Then I'll see you later.'

On days when Jeni went straight home from work, she did not bother changing out of uniform. Today she had planned to shop on her way home and had brought clothes to change into. Not glamorous gear, but better than a uniform, she thought, as she wriggled into jeans, critically surveying her trim waist and thighs in the full-length mirror in the change-room. And the red, over-sized cotton top looked chic enough with a white silk scarf knotted around her throat. She let her hair down from the roll she usually wore on duty and combed it vigorously, then made sure that her sun-glasses, large, white-framed, were handy in the top of her big white leather bag.

Outside, the sun was shining brilliantly, and she popped the sunglasses on. She had parked her car in shade that morning, but it had been standing in the sun for hours now, and a blast of hot air struck her as she opened the door. She wound down all the windows and stood for a moment or two, allowing the cooler air outside to circulate inside the car.

A slight breeze rustled the leaves of the trees behind her. She could smell the tang of the Harbour and hear the noisy horn of a ferry. She breathed deeply once or twice, trying to get rid of a small knot of nervousness, before slipping behind the wheel and driving the short distance round to the front of the Clinic building.

Marc Adams was waiting as she pulled into the kerb. He smiled as he opened the door and folded his long legs into the passenger seat.

'I could hardly have missed you,' he chuckled.

'I warned you,' Jeni said ruefully, as she checked her mirror and pulled out into the road.

'I didn't mean the car,' he protested. 'I have a fondness for Volkswagens—I used to have one myself. But the registration plate! Jeni-00! Is it Jeni-oooh or Jeni-oh! oh!?'

She laughed. 'Please yourself—as long as you don't think me horribly egotistical! I'd never have bought personalised plates, but some friends from the hospital gave them to me on my twenty-first birthday. My father says they're probably worth more than the car.'

'I hate to say it, but he could be right,' said Marc.

'Well, I did suggest he buy me a new car, since I'm his only daughter.'

'Are you an only child?' he asked.

'No. I have three older brothers.'

'Who no doubt spoil you rotten. Your father was probably wise not to compound the felony by giving you a new car.'

'I don't think that was the reason. He seemed to feel he might be donating the car to his future son-in-law.'

'Oh? And wouldn't *he* be deserving of a new car?'

'As yet, he exists mainly in my parents' imagination,' Jeni assured him.

He said, 'Oh,' again and Jeni thought she detected a note of relief in his voice. Her imagination must be running riot! Of course, if he were not married, the trend of their conversation would have been rather embarrassing. But, since he was married, there could be no such connotations.

As they talked, she had been making her way skilfully through heavy late-afternoon traffic. Now, as she stopped at a traffic light, she felt his eyes on her and turned her head to meet his gaze. They exchanged a smile but said nothing, but, as the light turned green and she drove on, she was very much aware of him at her side.

He was looking around him with interest.

'This is fascinating,' he said. 'I was expecting typical urban build-up, but these steep gullies look like virgin bush—as though they haven't changed since early settlement.'

'Much of the North Shore is like this. Sydney has its fair share of surburban sprawl, though, like any city. Have you found somewhere permanent to live yet?' she asked, thinking that she knew so little about him.

'I have an apartment in Kirribilli—on loan from a friend who's on a twelve-month sabbatical in the UK.'

'That's convenient to both the hospital and the city,' she remarked.

'Yes.'

An apartment was fine for him, but when his family arrived they would need something more in the way of accommodation. It was on the tip of her tongue to suggest that his first priority should be to find a house, rather than a school—he probably did not know that houses in Sydney, either for rent or sale, were as scarce as hens' teeth. But they were approaching a school she wanted him to see, so she filed the question away in her mind for later and slowed down, as much as she could in the flow of traffic, as he gazed intently in the direction she indicated.

An hour later, they had seen the outside of three

more schools and Jeni had told Marc what she knew of
each. He eliminated two, for various reasons, and
added the names and locations of the other one to the
two he already had in his small notebook.

'I'll ring tomorrow and arrange for interviews with
their admissions staff,' he said.

Jeni was intent on finding a gap in the traffic to
change lanes, and missed another opportunity to talk
to him about housing. And really, she thought, it was
not her business—he might already have the matter
well in hand.

'Shall I drop you back at the Clinic?' she asked him.

'If it's not too far out of your way?'

'Not at all.'

Her dashboard clock was showing five-fifteen. She
would leave her other shopping for today, and just pick
up some essentials for her evening meal, nearer home.

But Marc Adams had other ideas. As she stopped
the car outside the Clinic, he said, 'In return for your
help this afternoon, I should very much like to take
you out for a meal somewhere, if you're free.'

'I'm free. But it's not necessary. I'm happy to have
been of use.'

'Nevertheless, I'd be pleased if you'd come.'

The lift of her heart told her that she had not wanted
this afternoon to come to an end so soon. There was
no reason why she should not extend it by accepting
his invitation.

'Thank you, that would be lovely,' she smiled. 'I'll
have to change, though.'

'What time shall I pick you up?'

'Say seven?'

'Great. I'll be there at seven.' He sounded as elated
as she was feeling. Then he laughed. 'I'll be *where* at
seven?'

Jeni laughed too. 'Good thinking! I'll leave my street directory with you.'

She reached across to take the directory from the glove compartment. He leaned forward at the same instant, with the same intention, and, for a second, their heads were within an inch or two of one another. A whiff of aftershave stirred Jeni's senses. She jerked back into her seat and waited for him to pass the directory to her.

He did so, looking at her and smiling. 'That's not the first time we almost bumped heads while reaching for the same article.'

'Heathrow,' she said. 'I'm glad you've forgiven me for that.'

He looked surprised. 'What was there to forgive?'

She shrugged. 'I don't know, but you did seem rather upset about it at the time. I almost wondered whether you suspected me of trying to purloin your bag.'

'I'm sorry if I appeared rude. I had. . .other things on my mind.'

He did not elucidate further, but watched as she found the page in the directory.

'This is where we are now. And this,' turning a page, 'is where my apartment is. Top floor. Turn right at the top of the stairs, second door on right.'

It took her longer than usual to drive to Manly. Every traffic light seemed to be red and traffic on the other side of the Spit Bridge was moving at a snail's pace. She eventually discovered that the hold-up was being caused by a collection of ambulances, police cars and tow trucks at the scene of an accident, which were blocking two of the three available traffic lanes.

She showered quickly and dressed in a pale butter-cup-yellow frock with a full skirt and tiny sleeves. She would have washed her hair had she had time, but, with its natural wave, that was never really a problem. When the doorbell rang, she was putting careful, quite unnecessary touches to her eye make-up.

She had to restrain herself from dancing across the floor to open the door. It was the frock, she told herself—it was made for dancing.

Marc looked at her approvingly when she opened the door.

'Nice!' he said.

He too had a freshly scrubbed and groomed look, though he was still wearing the same suit. He had probably showered at the Clinic but had not had time to go home to Kirribilli to change.

'Shall we have a drink before we go?' she asked, then added, 'I'm rather keen to show you the view from my balcony.' As soon as she had said it she flushed, thinking that it sounded too much like a 'come up and see my etchings' suggestion.

He seemed not to notice her confusion but said, 'Yes, to both.'

Jeni poured drinks and they took them through on to the small balcony which was exclusively hers. Marc exclaimed as he looked from left to right.

'Lovely! And this, of course, is ocean—not Harbour?'

'Yes. If there were a window in that wall,' pointing in the opposite direction, 'we could see the Harbour. Manly is on an isthmus, with the sea on one side and the Harbour on the other, and only a few minutes' walk between the two.'

He sighed. 'I'm reluctant to drag myself away. I'd settle for a sandwich right here.'

'I should have thought of that myself. I could still rustle up something.'

'No!' he protested. 'I'm looking forward too much to

taking you out. And I have reservations at a restaurant Bill recommended, at a place called the Rocks. I hope he's reliable.'

'The Rocks has any number of fascinating eating-places,' said Jeni. 'Bill looks like a man who would know about such things.'

In the street, Marc opened the door of a dark-grey Alfa sedan and settled her in the passenger seat.

'My friend's car,' he explained.

'You'll have to introduce me to your friend when he gets back from the UK,' laughed Jeni.

'Oh, you wouldn't like him. . .he's far too old!'

'I like his taste in cars.'

He smiled at her. 'We'll do better if you navigate. Other than between the hospital and Kirribilli I tend to lose myself rather easily.'

'The Rocks is an area practically under the pylon at the southern end of the Bridge,' she told him. 'Actually, it's where the first working party of convicts landed on Australian soil. It's been called the Rocks ever since.'

The drive into the city seemed to take no time at all. As they approached the Bridge, heavy black thunder-clouds were gathering overhead.

'We often get these late afternoon storms,' Jeni said.

Once over the Bridge, she was kept busy directing Marc through labyrinthine streets to a restaurant in an old converted pier on the western side of Circular Quay.

They were given a table by a window with a view across the water. The water had taken on a sombre grey hue from the clouds overhead and lights were beginning to spring up in office blocks in North Sydney and on the water. Most of the craft moving to and fro were ferries, carrying home city workers.

Even as Marc and Jeni watched, a shaft of light from the westering sun broke through the clouds and, like a laser beam, unerringly alighted on the Opera House across the Cove, picking out and illuminating the soaring white contours of its sail-like roof, so that it looked like a giant galleon, afloat on a dark sea.

'That's really something!' Marc breathed, enthralled.

Jeni, feeling a proprietorial sense of pride, could only nod.

They conferred over menus and decided on seafood, with Sydney Rock oysters, blue swimmer crabs, prawns and scallops. As they toyed with drinks while waiting for their meal to be served, Jeni asked, 'What made you come to Australia?'

It was no more than a conversational gambit, but his response startled her. His face became closed and tense, his brows drawn together as he said tightly, 'My reasons were personal.'

Jeni felt her face redden. 'I'm sorry! I didn't mean to intrude. I only. . .' She stopped in confusion.

He made an effort to smile. 'And I didn't mean to be rude.'

He fingered his fork, looking down at the table. When he looked up at her, his eyes, though still shadowed as if haunted by some memory, seemed to be asking her for forgiveness and understanding.

With a palpable effort, he said, 'This wine is really excellent. If the meal is as good, Bill will go up a rung or two in my estimation.'

Jeni made an effort, too, to keep the conversation moving until the awkward moment had passed, and she resolved to ask no more personal questions. Perhaps when. . .if. . .she got to know him better, he would volunteer to tell her about himself and whatever it was in his past that had the power to affect him so.

She brought the subject round to their impressions of the hospital, and shop talk carried them through the remainder of the meal. The seafood was delectable, and freshly baked bread, still hot from the oven, was the perfect accompaniment.

Halfway through their meal, the storm broke outside. Lightning flashed and thunder crackled, then rain came down in torrents. By the time they left the restaurant, it had cleared and everything was clean and sparkling. The night air was fresh and cool as they drove back across the Bridge with the windows down. It seemed to blow away the last vestige of the constraint caused by Marc's earlier outburst.

They had not lingered too long over their meal, knowing that they both had to work tomorrow. When Marc stopped the car outside Jeni's apartment block, it was not quite ten o'clock.

'Thank you for a lovely evening,' she said, as they stood beside the car.

'Thank *you* for your help this afternoon,' adding, 'I'll see you to your door.'

They were silent as they climbed the stairs and walked along the passage to her flat. She felt in her handbag for her key, knowing that she did not want this evening to end.

'Would you like another cup of coffee? Or a liqueur?' she asked.

'Yes, that would be lovely.'

She opened the door and reached a hand for the light switch. Marc followed her into the living-room. It was a large L-shaped room, with a small dining setting inside the sliding door which led to the balcony. There were three rattan easy chairs and a large settee, a coffee-table, a TV and video-cassette recorder. A small kitchen opened off the living-room, and a short passageway led to the two bedrooms.

Marc closed the door behind him. He stood, not moving into the room, but looking at Jeni. And what she saw in his eyes made her heart pound, suffocatingly, in her throat.

'Jeni!' he breathed.

She was completely unprepared for this, completely vulnerable.

His arms were around her, drawing her to him. His mouth found hers and she opened her lips to the demand of his. She could feel his body, hard and strong, against hers and she melted against him, knowing that she had been waiting for this all evening. No, for much longer than that—ever since she had met him on the plane. She felt as though she was being carried away on a wave of bliss and losing touch with reality. She had never in her life felt like this, and she wanted it to go on for ever.

His hands moving down her back, forcing her even more closely to him, brought her to her senses. This man she was surrendering to without so much as a token resistance was married—and had two children.

It was the memory of the children that won the battle for her. She had only the dimmest recollection of his wife, in the lounge at Heathrow, and he had said nothing to make her more flesh-and-blood to Jeni. But the children—she could visualise them vividly, could see them in their father's arms, kissing him goodbye. And he had talked about them—he and she had spent that very afternoon looking for schools for them. They were real, and they were young and defenceless. For their sakes, this must not be allowed to go any further, however much she longed for it to do just that.

She thrust her hands against his chest and forced her

face back, away from his. She had to turn her head to escape his still-searching lips, but she managed to articulate, 'No, Marc! No!'

He became very still, and slowly, as she continued to resist, his arms loosened their hold and fell to his sides. She stepped back and looked at him, then spoke through lips that felt bruised from his kisses.

'Why did you have to do that?' she asked.

His face was pale now, and wiped clean of expression. He ran a hand through his hair and distract-edly moved a few paces into the room.

'I'm sorry,' he said. 'I shouldn't have. . .it was too soon.'

'It will always be too soon,' she said. 'I'll never. . .'

There was a knock on the door and the sound of a key being inserted into the lock.

Jeni just had time to sink into an armchair. Marc followed her lead and, when the door opened, they were both sitting, their heads turned towards the door, as if they had been interrupted in the middle of a conversation.

'Liz!' Jeni exclaimed, and was thankful her voice sounded reasonably normal. 'I wasn't expecting you tonight. Tony—hi!'

'I tried to ring but got no answer,' Liz explained. 'I thought perhaps you'd been changed to a p.m. shift. Tony offered to run me out and I decided to take a chance on there being a bed for me.'

'We've been out. Liz, this is Marc Adams. We met on the plane from London. Marc, this is Liz, an old fellow trainee. And Tony—Marc Adams.'

She had contrived to make the introductions without actually looking at Marc. Liz glanced curiously from Jeni to Marc, but Tony seemed to have noticed nothing out of the ordinary. He showed no signs of being upset that she had been out with another man.

He turned to Jeni and explained, 'Liz and I have both had a heavy day—a string of minor emergencies, topped off by a haemoptysis. Liz was so worn out, I took pity on her and offered to drive her out here so she can sleep in in the morning, which is just about impossible in the nurses' home—but I don't have to tell *you* that.'

Liz, with her jet-black hair, deep blue eyes and flawless alabaster complexion, was looking particularly attractive tonight, even in her uniform. And not at all exhausted, Jeni thought. Certainly not as exhausted as she herself was beginning to feel. Resisting Marc seemed to have completely drained her of strength.

She sat for a moment more, listening to the others talk. Tony was always an easy conversationalist, and he already had Marc admitting his ignorance about sailing and drawing Tony out on what was so obviously his favourite subject.

Jeni forced herself to stand up. 'Coffee all round?' she asked.

There was a murmur of assent, and Liz followed her into the kitchen and helped assemble mugs, coffee-pot, biscuits.

'Did Tony stop for tea?' Jeni asked Liz, knowing that it was often not possible for RMOs to do so when there was a rush on.

'I doubt it. It wasn't that kind of day.'

Jeni poked her head around the door to ask, 'Do you need something more substantial than biscuits, Tony?'

'Do I ever! As long as it's not one of Charlene's leftover creations.'

'Ham and cheese croissants?'

'Just what the doctor ordered! How about you, Marc? Or do you lead a more civilised existence in your private hospital?'

'We've been very civilised tonight. We went to a superb restaurant in the city—at the Rocks. A fascinating area. . .'

Their voices went on. Jeni could hear only a word here and there as she and Liz chattered in the kitchen. She wondered that Marc could sound so relaxed and normal. Perhaps he was more accustomed than she was to scenes such as they had just been through. The thought didn't please her at all.

As she and Liz carried the supper into the living-room, Tony was saying, 'Right! That's settled, then!' Turning to the two girls, he said, 'I've invited Marc to come out in the boat one day soon. If you girls could arrange your days off to suit, we could all go.'

It was a typical Tony suggestion, impulsive, spur-of-the-moment. But, as so often happened with his suggestions, they were all able, after some discussion, to say that yes, they were able to make it this coming Saturday, which was Tony's day off.

The discussion about arrangements went back and forth. It became clear to Jeni that Tony and Liz had already known that they were both off on Saturday. She registered the fact, but it did not seem particularly significant. Nothing seemed very significant just then. Her mind seemed to be in a sort of limbo—almost numb.

Sitting across the room, holding his mug of coffee and chatting casually, Marc seemed quite at ease and unaware of how she was feeling. But, a few moments later, catching his eye on her, she knew that he was not as composed as he seemed to be. His look was questioning, aware, concerned for her. It was almost her undoing.

When Tony had finished his croissant and a large slab of fruit cake, he carried the tray into the kitchen for Jeni. She had thought he was unaware of the tension between herself and Marc, but, as he placed the tray on the sink, he asked, 'Are you OK, mate? Do you want to talk about it?'

Quick, unexpected tears flooded her eyes and, turning towards him, she buried her head in his shoulder. He put his arms around her in a hug that was so comfortable and familiar that it gave her an answer which should satisfy him and stop more questions.

'I guess I'm a bit homesick for you all,' she confessed. 'I've seen so little of anyone since I've been back.'

Raising her head, she caught Marc watching them. He had moved across to the balcony window to look at the view, and they were standing in his direct line of vision, through the door to the kitchen.

He looked away quickly and moved back into the room. When she and Tony re-entered the living-room, Marc was standing talking to Liz and began immediately to take his departure. His leavetaking from Jeni was formal.

'Thank you for a lovely dinner,' she said.

'My pleasure. See you Saturday, Tony, Liz.'

And he was gone.

CHAPTER FOUR

WITH the departure of the men, the flat seemed suddenly empty.

Jeni was thankful that Liz showed no inclination to sit up talking, so they tidied up quickly, said goodnight and went to bed.

For an hour, Jeni alternately pummelled her pillow and tried to force herself to relax. But sleep eluded her. Finally she gave up and quietly, so as not to disturb Liz, crept out and switched on the television, with the sound-level very low. She stared blankly at an old black and white movie for a time, without beginning to take in the story, then switched it off and sat looking out at a dark ocean and listening to the intermittent whisper of waves on the beach. The lights of a cargo ship, far out, were moving slowly across the horizon.

She did not try to hide from herself that Marc's kisses had awoken in her a passion that she was going to find impossible to ignore. At least the question of Tony was settled, once and for all, because she had never felt anything like this for Tony.

Then she became angry with Marc. What right had he to shatter all her comfortable expectations for the future? What was he looking for from her? A casual dalliance in his wife's absence? A more permanent relationship of which his wife was to be kept in ignorance?

She tried to encourage her feelings of anger. It was the only way she could keep in check the ridiculous, irrepressible little bubble of joy which kept intruding into her thinking and rising to the surface. She reminded herself that there was simply nothing in this situation to be happy about. Except that Marc, whatever his intentions, had liked her enough to kiss her.

The lights of the cargo ship had disappeared past the Point before she stood up and went back to bed.

Before falling asleep, she made one final resolution. When she saw Marcus Adams on duty her attitude towards him would be strictly professional. She would accept no more invitations from him, however innocuous they seemed to be. It was not that she could not trust him. It was that she knew her feelings could play her false again, as they had last night.

She would, of course, have to see him on Saturday, but there would be others there then, and she would take good care that she and Marc were not alone together.

On duty that morning she had to force herself to concentrate on the night sister's report, but only for a minute or two. The night sister's name was Harry. He was six feet tall and ruggedly built and his report was a masterpiece, crisp and precise, and to it he added humorous, off-the-cuff comments. A nice guy, she thought, and wondered whether she would have the chance to get to know him better.

Collecting a bundle of linen for her first bed-make, she wondered whether today was going to be as ho-hum as the previous two days had been. She could do with some excitement today to take her mind off. . .other things. But, in a hospital which had no casualty unit to provide the unexpected, and where most of the surgery was elective, ward duty would be pretty much routine.

She had only four patients on her list today. Two of

these were ready for discharge, and she decided to attend to them first. Paula Brown was in the shower. Jeni tapped on the door, called, 'Good morning,' over the sound of running water, then made up the bed and tidied the room without seeing her patient. Next was Mrs Petersen, a tiny, faded but still pretty woman, who had had surgery for a primary cancer of the thyroid gland, which had been completely successful. This morning she was dressed and sitting in an armchair with the *Sydney Morning Herald* on her knees.

'Hello, Mrs Petersen. Looking forward to going home tomorrow?' asked Jeni.

Mrs Petersen looked anything but pleased at the prospect. 'Do you really think I'm well enough?' she replied.

'Your doctor must think so, or he wouldn't be letting you go.'

Mrs Petersen said nothing, but looked back down at her paper. A little later, Jeni noticed that she was biting her lower lip and that her eyes, fixed on the printed page, were not moving. There was something here that needed looking into. Jeni resolved to come back later when she had more time and find out what was troubling her patient.

Her next patient, an elderly man, admitted for investigation of gall-bladder colic and possible surgery, was still in bed and dozing when Jeni entered. He stirred and opened his eyes.

'Don't bother to wake up,' said Jeni. 'I'll make your bed later, while you're in Radiography. Remember not to eat or drink anything before that, won't you?'

'Uh-huh.'

So far, so good. She was ahead of schedule, and it was just as well, because her next patient was Mrs Jackson, who had been most petulant and demanding since her partial gastrectomy three days ago—Marcus Adams' first case in the hospital. She had been told before her operation that she would be on an intravenous drip and suction post-operatively, but seemed quite unable to accept that they were routine procedures for her type of surgery and did not mean she was seriously ill. She made no secret of the fact that she thought the nurses were being cruelly sadistic when they insisted she move around her room at regular intervals, despite the paraphernalia to which she was attached. She was a time-consuming patient who required the patience of a saint to care for.

She was sound asleep when Jeni entered her room. Jeni quietly checked the flow rate of the IV and noted the strong, regular pulse beating in Mrs Jackson's neck. She was showing no sign of discomfort. Perhaps the morning blanket bath would not be such a trying experience this morning. Jeni slipped away to the utility-room and loaded up a trolley with everything she would need for the bath.

When she returned, Mrs Jackson was stirring.

'Good morning, Mrs Jackson,' Jeni said cheerily.

'Hello, Nurse.'

It was the policy of the hospital that patients use the Christian names of staff members, but Mrs Jackson seemed to have a problem with this, so Jeni had not insisted. Neither had she reminded Mrs Jackson that she was 'Sister' and not 'Nurse'.

As Jeni stripped the bed deftly, leaving one warm blanket in place, she chattered away, saying it was a lovely day outside and perhaps Mrs Jackson could walk as far as the balcony later on and watch the boats on the Harbour for a while. No reply was forthcoming. Jeni rinsed a face-cloth in warm water for Mrs Jackson to wash her face, then handed her a towel. But when it came to sponging her arms, Mrs Jackson assumed a stubborn expression which Jeni knew presaged a comment to the effect that this was what she was paying the nurses to do for her. Eventually she accepted the cloth again and moved it languidly over her hands and forearms, before dropping it and saying, faintly, 'Really, Nurse, I must have something for the pain. Doctor said I don't have to suffer like this.'

Jeni doubted that Marcus Adams had worded it just like that, but she said, 'You can have something if you need it. I'll go and get you a tablet.'

'A tablet? I've been having injections!'

'Doctor wants you to try a tablet today, now that you're off the suction,' Jeni explained.

'Oh, well! I'll try it if he said so, but I know it won't work.'

'Are your arms quite dry?'

Mrs Jackson shrugged and turned her head away. Jeni pulled the blanket up under her chin and, although the morning was not cold, tucked a pink bedjacket round her shoulders as well.

'OK?' she asked brightly, adding, 'I'll be back in just a moment.'

It took more than a moment. Jeni had to find Helen to get the keys to the drug cupboard, return to the duty-room, extract the fifty-milligram Pethidine tablet from the cupboard in the corner of the room, enter it in the drug book, chart it in the case-notes and then return the keys to Helen who would, at the same time, check the drug.

She had got as far as writing the medication in the drug book, with the tablet on a tiny paper plate beside her on the desk, when the code bell rang.

Someone was having a cardiac arrest!

Helen and she were the only trained staff on duty.

They would be responsible for resuscitation procedures until a medical team arrived. The first thing to be done was to summon that team. The phone was at Jeni's hand, and she quickly dialled Switchboard, said, 'Code Blue. Surgical Two,' as soon as they answered, and hung up. Switchboard would know which doctors were in the hospital and would call two of them on their beepers.

The Doctor Blue case, containing essential equipment for use in an emergency like this, was in the duty-room. Jeni grabbed it and was almost out of the door when she remembered the Pethidine tablet on the table. She shoved it hastily between the pages of the drug book and pushed the book far back on the table. Then she sped out of the room.

A red light was showing over the door of the room where she had found Helen only minutes earlier. Anne Morrow's room! So it was Anne who had arrested! Thank goodness Helen had been on the spot and would have started resuscitation immediately. That would certainly be in Anne's favour.

Sure enough, when Jeni arrived Anne was already receiving oxygen through an oral airway, with a nurse at her head, supporting her jaw. Helen had begun cardiac compression but, seeing the case in Jeni's hands, nodded to her to take over the compression, while she herself began preparing to establish an intra-venous line.

Jeni had done cardiac compression many times before, in mock arrests during her training and in real emergencies like this one. Placing the heels of her hands, one on top of the other, on the lower half of Anne's chest and keeping her fingers raised, she began to press and release, depress and release. . .

When, minutes later, two doctors arrived, they

nodded approval of what the girls had done. It needed another five minutes, the injection of a cardiac stimulant and the use of the paddles to have Anne's heart beating rhythmically again and everyone in the room breathing freely.

Anne was transferred to Intensive Care, where she would be put on a monitor. Helen, whose patient she was, went with her and Jeni was free to return to her own duties. It took a moment to remember what she had been doing when the interruption occurred. Oh, yes—Mrs Jackson's Pethidine. She sped back to the duty-room. The drug book was still lying on the table. She opened it. The little paper plate was still there. But the tablet had gone!

Jeni stared in disbelief. It was not possible! Perhaps it had somehow become dislodged. She searched the table, then went on hands and knees beneath it. But in vain.

Misplacing a dangerous drug was a serious offence. Jeni felt sick. She would have to report the loss as soon as possible—as soon as Helen returned to the ward. In the meantime, she must get back to Mrs Jackson, who had probably worked herself into a state waiting for her medication.

Jeni still had the keys of the drug cupboard pinned to the inside of her pocket where she had put them until she could return them to Helen. She opened the cupboard, extracted another tablet, made another entry in the book immediately under the last one, locked the cupboard and went quickly to Mrs Jackson's room.

As she approached the partly closed door, she could hear Mrs Jackson's voice, but could not make out what she was saying. Perhaps one of the nurses had used her initiative, knowing that Jeni was occupied with the arrest, and had carried on sponging Mrs Jackson. But when Mrs Jackson's voice stopped, it was a man's voice that replied. Jeni's heart skipped a beat as she recognised the voice. Marcus Adams! Why was he in the ward so early? Perhaps he had a long OR list and had decided to see his ward patients first.

She hesitated outside the door, reluctant to face him after what had happened last night. Her cheeks flamed at the memory. And it did nothing for her equanimity to realise that Mrs Jackson had been complaining to him about the treatment she had been receiving from her nurse that morning. As she stood hesitating to walk into the room, her suspicions about the subject of their conversation were confirmed when she heard Marc say, 'Yes, of course. I shall speak to the sister in charge about this.'

Jeni felt her legs go weak with anger. She could understand and forgive Mrs Jackson, who was simply reacting, in a fairly predictable way, to her hospital experience. She had been uprooted from her comfortable home, where she was used to being the centre of her small universe, and transplanted into hospital where she was only one of many requiring the attention of the staff. She had been subjected to all sorts of traumas and indignities. Her tantrums and complaining were her way of dealing with the situation—she was trying to pull everything and everyone into orbit about herself so that she could feel secure in the presence of so much that was strange and threatening.

All this Jeni understood and was trained to cope with. It was Marc Adams' perfidy that kept her standing there in stunned disbelief.

There was an unwritten law, in hospitals, that doctors and nurses stood up for one another—covered for one another in situations like this. Even if a nurse was guilty of some dereliction of duty, it was never mentioned in front of a patient. The patient needed to have confidence in the entire medical team who were taking care of her, not to have that confidence undermined. And a nurse, likewise, although she might sometimes doubt the wisdom of a doctor's treatment, and might even say so to him, would never let a patient suspect that she had those reservations.

All that Marc needed to have said in response to Mrs Jackson's complaints was that there must have been some good reason why Sister had been delayed. Instead he was agreeing with Mrs Jackson that she had been treated badly.

Jeni did not wait to hear any more. Taking a deep breath to quell her indignation, she opened the door fully, stepped into the room and said, 'Good morning, Doctor.'

He swung round at the sound of her voice. There was a long pause before he replied, 'Sister!' He looked at her intently, as if trying to find something in her face, but, not finding it, his eyes hardened and his face became as closed and remote as her own. Jeni knew that her expression reflected what felt like a cold, heavy lump of lead inside her.

After another long pause, during which he seemed uncertain what to say, he turned to Mrs Jackson. 'I'll be back to see you later, my dear, when you're more comfortable. I'll see you later too, Sister.' His words had an ominous ring.

'Yes, Doctor.' He was gone, and Jeni moved to the locker beside Mrs Jackson.

'I'm sorry I had to leave you for so long,' she said. 'Here's your tablet. Just a mouthful or two of water with it—that's fine! Now I'll finish sponging you as quickly as I can and you'll be nice and comfortable.'

It wasn't only for Mrs Jackson's benefit that she must be quick. She must report the loss of the Pethidine as soon as she possibly could.

She prattled lightly as she worked. 'I'll change your bedlinen later, when you're up having your walk. It's been a miserable few days for you, I know, but I promise, from now on things will improve. Would you like the hairdresser to come this morning? You have such pretty hair, and I'm sure it'll make you feel better when your family visit you this afternoon.'

Gradually Mrs Jackson's face lost its sulky, shame-faced expression, and, as Jeni put the final tidying touches to the room, she said, in a subdued voice, 'Thank you, Nurse. . .and. . . I'm sorry.'

Jeni reassured her. 'We've both had a bad start to the day. Let's forget about it and have a good day from now on. Is that tablet helping the pain yet?'

'Yes, thank you, Jeni.'

Eureka! thought Jeni. Progress! She flashed her patient a wide, all-pals-together grin. 'Don't mention it,' she said.

But as she wheeled her trolley back to the utility-room and cleared it away, her optimism evaporated and she knew that her bad day had only just begun.

She found Helen sitting at the table in the duty-room, engrossed in paperwork. Jeni guessed she was writing the report on Anne Morrow's cardiac arrest.

'Can it wait?' she said to Jeni, without looking up.

'I'm afraid not.'

At the seriousness of Jeni's tone, Helen looked up, put down her pen and asked, 'What is it?'

Jeni explained in as few words as possible about the missing Pethidine. Helen whistled softly through her teeth.

'Phew! You have no idea where it might have gone?'

'Absolutely none.'

'You didn't see anyone near here at the time?'

'No. But I was intent on getting in to help you with the CA. I probably wouldn't have noticed if there *had* been anyone round.'

They were both silent, thinking deeply.

Jeni said, 'I'm worried that it may have been a patient who wandered in and took it. We have a couple of them who are non-compos enough to do that. And if someone for whom it wasn't intended took it, it could have adverse effects. Shall I do a full TPR round now—not just the usual four-hourlies—and watch out for anything abnormal—slowed pulse or respirations, change in pupil size, whatever?'

'Good thought. Do it stat. And I'll. . .you do realise that I'll have to report this to Matron?'

'Of course.' The thought made Jeni's spirits drop even lower, if that were possible.

She did her TPR round, carefully taking each patient's temperature and counting pulse and respiration rates. Most of the patients accepted this aberration of their normal routine without comment. A few expressed surprise. 'Again? Nurse has only just taken it.'

'Oh, well! A little extra practice never goes amiss for us nurses.'

Or, 'Am I all right, Sister? I didn't think I had a temperature.'

'You're fine! Just my way of getting to know the patients.'

'Of course! You're new here, aren't you?'

Once or twice she had to resort to manoeuvring to get patients into a position where she could check their pupil size without them knowing what she was doing.

Her round finished, she returned to the duty-room.

'Any joy?' asked Helen, looking up hopefully from her work.

'Not a thing. Nothing that doesn't correspond with the night report, or with medication that's been given since.'

'Do you think it's possible that a practical joker. . .?'

Jeni shook her head. 'Who knows?' After a moment she went on, 'Helen, have you wondered whether *I* might have taken it? After all, I'm new—you don't know me very well. . .'

'Absolutely not! I reject that idea out of hand.' Helen sighed heavily and stood up. 'Well, I can't put off reporting to Matron any longer.' She glanced into the mirror on the wall above the table and put a hand up to her hair. 'I shouldn't be off the floor more than ten or fifteen minutes. Nurse Clarke is with Mr Burchell in Room Seven. His vital signs are OK: BP a hundred and twelve over seventy-eight, pulse seventy-two, respirations fifteen. He was agitated earlier and is to remain in soft restraints as long as he's intubated. But he's responding to voices and moving his limbs on command.'

Mr Burchell had been admitted two hours earlier following a cerebral haemorrhage. He had been intubated and was having oxygen administered through a ventilator. As the only other trained nurse on duty, Jeni would be in charge of the floor during Helen's absence.

Helen departed, and Jeni poked her head around the door of Room Seven, receiving a reassuring nod from Nurse Clarke that all was well. As she returned along the corridor, she was intercepted by a delivery boy, carrying a large floral arrangement. Jeni took it from him, said, 'Thanks,' and looked at the card attached to it. Mrs Jackson. The flowers would be coals to Newcastle, because Mrs Jackson's room was already a floral bower. Still, this offering might do something to improve her patient's humour.

As she walked towards Mrs Jackson's room, a voice behind her said, 'May I have a word with you, Sister?'

Marc Adams. And being professionally formal. That was good. But, as she turned to face him, she saw something in his blue eyes that was other than professionalism and that threatened to upset her careful but fragile sangfroid.

She balanced the flowers, a tall arrangement in a shallow plastic bowl, carefully in front of her and regarded Marc with a wide, serious stare over the top of them, waiting for the reproof she knew he was about to administer.

Disconcertingly, his lips twitched and there was laughter in his eyes. Her own twinkled back at him momentarily, acknowledging that she must look slightly ridiculous—a bride in a starched white uniform with a huge bouquet. When he spoke, her smile vanished, because she knew that he was not about to declare a truce after all.

'I told Mrs Jackson I'd speak to you this morning.'

Suddenly Jeni was furious. It was thanks to him that she had come on duty this morning feeling tired and tense. Since then, there'd been the war of attrition with Mrs Jackson, Anne Morrow's arrest and the loss of the Pethidine. Now she was being confronted by a doctor who was about to accuse her of neglecting her patient, without bothering to find out what had caused her prolonged absence from Mrs Jackson's room. Well, she would have her say first.

She kept her voice low, in case there were inadvertent eavesdroppers behind the closed doors nearby. But her words lost nothing in emphasis.

'I know Mrs Jackson talked to you this morning—complained to you. I happened to arrive back in time to hear what you said to her. Apparently you're prepared to condemn me out of hand, without knowing why I left her alone for so long.'

He looked completely taken back, and made as if to interrupt her. But she gave him no chance and plunged on.

'We have a code of ethics in Australia which says that doctors and nurses support one another, cover up for one another, if necessary, to a patient, not make things worse by agreeing with their criticisms. Perhaps things are different in England, but here. . .'

'I'd leave it there, if I were you!'

His voice too was low and controlled, but it cut like a whiplash across her tirade, so that she forgot what she was about to say and stood, open-mouthed and astonished.

'Now listen to me!. . .and put those ridiculous flowers down! Here, give them to me!'

He took them from her, walked a few steps and stood them, very carefully, on an elegant cabriole-legged half-table which already bore a large bowl of roses. That done, he turned and faced her.

'I think I've got the gist of what you're saying—and you're dead wrong! Yes, Mrs Jackson *did* complain about her treatment, at some length, and, to be honest, I was inclined to think she had something to complain about. But I did *not*—emphatically *not*—agree with her that she'd been badly treated.'

'But I heard you say. . .' Jeni hesitated, trying to remember his exact words.

'You heard me say what?'

'That you intended speaking to Sister about it.'

'Then all I can say is that you must have had a very

guilty conscience, to jump to the conclusion that I intended to lodge a complaint against you,' he said, with the faintest hint of a smile creasing his lips.

Furious, she opened her mouth with a sharp intake of breath. But Marc forestalled her again.

'*You* were the sister I intended speaking to, but just then didn't seem to be the appropriate time, with Mrs Jackson lying naked under her blanket.'

He held up a hand as she attempted to interrupt again.

'I know, I know! You were helping with a cardiac arrest. I didn't know it at the time, but I *did* suggest to Mrs J. that you'd probably been held up by some emergency, and reminded her that if she herself had been in need of extra help after her surgery, everyone would have dropped what they were doing to come to her aid. I was careful to suggest that she was no longer likely to need such aid. Now, what else were you going to say?'

He had completely taken the wind out of her sails. Jeni stood there, feeling utterly deflated. What could she say? She *could* apologise. She *should* apologise.

Instead she heard herself saying, 'Just that I hate smug, self-satisfied Englishmen.'

Immediately she was horrified at herself and rushed into the apology she should have made.

'I'm sorry! I really am. I shouldn't have said that. I shouldn't have said anything. But it's been a bad morning. . .' Her voice faltered.

'After a bad night, perhaps?' His voice was very gentle now. 'I should be the one apologising. I didn't have a chance to say anything last night before the others came. But I *am* sorry I upset you, because I really did enjoy our dinner, and I'm grateful for your help with the schools.'

She nodded. 'I enjoyed it too.' His kindness was almost her undoing. She felt her throat constrict and sudden tears burn behind her eyes. Hastily, to get back on safe ground, she asked, 'What was it you wanted to speak to me about?'

'Apart from apologising about last night, I was going to tell you that I'd suggested to Mrs Jackson that she might be happier, at this stage of her convalescence, sharing a room with someone else, rather than dwelling on her miseries all alone. I didn't put it quite like that, though,' he smiled.

Jeni smiled back and nodded. 'It's a good idea. It would have to be somebody compatible, and someone strong enough to cope with Mrs Jackson without letting her whingeing get her down.'

'Is there such a person?'

'The ideal one would have been Anne Morrow.'

'She's gone home?' he queried.

'No. She's the one who had the cardiac arrest this morning.'

'I see. What a pity! Is there anyone else. . .?'

'Leave it to me,' said Jeni. 'I'll discuss it with Helen and see what we can come up with.'

As she moved away to pick up her flowers, he said quietly, 'Jeni.'

She turned to face him again. 'Yes?'

'You should have told me about Tony. He's special?'

She hadn't thought about Tony since he had left the apartment last evening. But, whatever her relationship with Tony was now, or was likely to be in the future, it had nothing to do with anything, as far as she and Marc Adams were concerned. At the same time, she could make use of it to resolve anything problematical that was likely to arise with Marc.

'Yes, he's special,' she said, and was about to add,

'And *you* should have told me about. . .' But she bit
back the words because she knew that she could not
have kept a revealing bitterness out of her voice.
Instead she said, 'Now, if you'll excuse me. . .'

For the second time that morning the emergency bell
rang—three short, urgent beeps.

Room Seven!

Jeni turned and sped in that direction, forgetting all
about Marc Adams, unaware even, that he was following her.

A single glance was sufficient to alert her to what
was happening in Room Seven. In his restlessness, and
in spite of the restraints on his arms, Mr Burchell had
managed to extubate himself—to remove the tube that
had been inserted in his trachea to facilitate his
breathing.

Nurse Clarke was standing beside her patient's bed,
looking horrified. As soon as she saw Jeni, she blurted
out, 'I only turned my back for a moment. . .!'

'Never mind that now,' said Jeni crisply. 'Help me
get him up into high Fowler's.'

Nurse Clarke was only too willing to do anything to
put to rights whatever damage had been done during
her moment of inattention to her patient. Experienced
as the two girls were, it was the work of less than a
minute to lift Mr Burchell's fourteen stone into an
upright position, supported by several pillows. As soon
as this was accomplished they both looked at him
anxiously, and breathed a collective sigh of relief to
note that his colour, which had been almost grey, was
improving perceptibly and the frightened look was
leaving his face.

'That's good, Mr Burchell. You're doing just fine,'
said Jeni reassuringly. 'Nurse will give you some more
oxygen through the mask, and that will help even

more.' She turned to Nurse Clarke and said, 'Forty per cent humidified.'

'Right.'

As Nurse Clarke adjusted the flow rate of oxygen and applied the mask to Mr Burchell's face, Jeni checked his pulse and respiration rates and then his blood-pressure, all of which were appreciably higher than what Helen had recorded earlier. But that was to be expected.

She turned to communicate her findings to Marc Adams.

Marc, on entering the room on Jeni's heels, had looked at once at the card above the bed, to ascertain the name of Mr Burchell's doctor, at the same time reaching for the phone. He spoke briefly to switchboard, then hung up and listened to Jeni's report of the patient's vital signs. He nodded, as though he found them satisfactory, then said quietly, 'You carry on, Sister.' Jeni realised that he was reluctant to interfere in another doctor's case until authorised to do so, but she found it reassuring to have him there. He would certainly intervene if Mr Burchell's condition deteriorated suddenly.

She spoke to Mr Burchell quietly. 'I'm going to take a blood sample now.' Another nurse materialised as Jeni got her sample and Jeni handed her the container, saying, 'Take this to the lab, stat, please, Nurse. For arterial blood gases.' Her calm, matter-of-fact tone belied the urgency of her request and was for Mr Burchell's benefit. The very worst thing for him, now, was to become agitated, as that could raise the pressure within his brain where the initial cerebro-vascular accident had occurred.

Jeni talked as she worked, explaining each thing she was doing. She checked the movement of his chest muscles. If these were exaggerated as he breathed in and out, it would indicate that his breathing was distressed, due perhaps to damage that had occurred to the tissues as the tube had been forcibly removed. If for any reason he was not receiving enough oxygen he could suffer further brain damage. It was a challenging situation and one that demanded of her the cool efficiency and medical know-how her training had instilled.

Mr Burchell attempted to speak, but his voice was hoarse and there was a gurgling noise in his throat. Jeni patted his hand. 'That's nothing to worry about—just a little bit of mucus.' She hoped very much that that was all it was. She looked across at Marc. 'Suction, do you think?'

He nodded, and lifted the receiver from the phone as it began to jangle. As he talked, he watched Jeni remove a suction tube from a bag hanging at the head of the bed and attach it to the outlet marked 'Suction' on the wall. 'Once I get rid of this from your throat, your breathing will be even easier,' she assured Mr Burchell.

Carefully, so as not to cause gagging, she inserted the tube, and a few moments later had the satisfaction of seeing a look of relief come over Mr Burchell's face. She felt as relieved as he. Apparently he had not done himself too much damage. If there had been much trauma or swelling to his throat and trachea he would not be breathing as easily as he now was. And his colour was definitely better.

Marc finished his phone conversation and moved across to the bed.

'Right!' he said, sounding relieved. 'Dr Stanislav is tied up in surgery. He's happy for me to look after you for a while, Mr Burchell, until he's free again, if that's

OK by you? By the way, I'm Marcus Adams—Dr Marcus Adams.'

Mr Burchell nodded, and Marc went on cheerfully, 'Not that these young ladies have left me much to do.'

Jeni was annoyed to find herself flushing at the look of approval he gave her. But she was pleased. This was the first time they had actually worked together—or she had worked and Marc had watched—and she knew that his approbation was very important to her.

She stepped back from the bed, nodding for Nurse Clarke to assist Dr Adams as he began his own examination of the patient.

Before long Helen arrived, having been alerted as to what had taken place during her absence. Jeni filled in the details for her, then entered them on Mr Burchell's case-notes, which Helen had brought with her.

Jeni's feeling of satisfaction at a job well done and a patient safely through what could have been a life-or-death crisis lasted until she had left the room and was standing in the corridor asking herself, 'Now, where was I?'

With a nasty jolt to her stomach she remembered the Pethidine and wondered how Matron had reacted to Helen's report. Well, she would have to wait to find out that until Helen was free. She picked up the flowers to be delivered to Mrs Jackson and walked along to her room.

'Look what I've got for you!' she said brightly. 'Someone must love you a lot!'

Mrs Jackson smiled tentatively. 'I'm beginning to realise I've got a lot to be thankful for after all. I'm sorry I've been such a sore-head.'

'Don't worry about it. It's all part of the process. We nurses make allowances for it after major surgery.'

Jeni was in Mrs Jackson's room again, later, trying

to entice her to eat the minuscule meal Marc had ordered for her, when Marc himself walked in. Mrs Jackson's face lit up. She was clearly thrilled to have a second, unscheduled visit from her handsome young surgeon. Jeni tried to hide the fact that her own reaction was somewhat similar to Mrs Jackson's.

It was only when Marc, after chatting pleasantly with his patient for a few minutes, turned to Jeni and said, 'Well done, Sister!' that she realised that it was she herself Marc had come to see, and that his 'Well done' did not refer to what she was doing for Mrs Jackson but to the earlier episode with Mr Burchell. She felt a sudden warmth around her heart and turned away so he would not see a certain mistiness in her eyes.

Marc had barely taken himself off when Helen hurried in, flustered and apologetic.

'I'm so sorry, Jeni! Matron wanted to see you at twelve o'clock, and it's now two minutes past.'

'Whew! I'd best fly!' gasped Jeni.

'Good luck!'

'Thanks.'

Matron was sitting behind her big table when Jeni arrived, apologising for being late. Matron nodded and motioned her to a chair on the other side of the table. She was middle-aged, tall and stately, with wings of white in her jet black hair, and piercing black eyes.

'Well, Sister. Tell me about the missing tablet.'

Jeni recounted succinctly what had happened that morning. When she had finished, Matron nodded thoughtfully.

'I've given this matter considerable thought,' she said. 'Whatever the truth of it is, the central fact is that a dangerous drug, for which you were responsible, is missing. The policy of the hospital is to deal decisively with any irregularity involving drugs. Firm action must be taken, and must be seen to be taken. Therefore I really have no option but to suspend you from your duties.'

Jeni could not suppress a gasp of dismay, but Matron held up a hand and continued, 'That doesn't mean that we believe you're guilty of having taken the tablet, although you must assume some responsibility for having left it as you did. I understand the circumstances, but nevertheless. . .' Matron paused and her silence was expressive.

'In telling you what I'm about to tell you, I'm taking you into my confidence and trusting you not to divulge it to anyone.'

Jeni wondered what was to come, and forced herself to unclasp her hands which had been tightly folded in her lap.

'Only two people other than myself know that we have reason to suspect that drugs have been. . . misappropriated recently. Whoever is responsible has covered their tracks very cleverly. We felt we were more likely to track down the culprit if we didn't reveal our suspicions to anyone. That's why there's been no public furore.'

Matron paused again, as though wondering whether to say more. Jeni sat and waited.

'It's just possible,' Matron said, 'that by directing suspicion in your direction, whoever is responsible will become less careful and show his—or her—hand. That, of course, is more likely to happen if you're on duty, so your suspension will be a token one only, lasting until, I think, Monday afternoon. That will include, of course, your rostered days off duty. Is there anything you'd like to ask me?'

Jeni was having so much difficulty adjusting her mind to this totally unexpected development that she could think of nothing to say. She shook her head. 'No, thank you, Matron.'

Matron's face relaxed into a smile. 'Then off you go. And enjoy your unscheduled holiday!'

'Thank you, Matron.'

'Thank *you*, Jeni, for being willing to co-operate.'

CHAPTER FIVE

SO MUCH for boring routine!

It was less than eight hours since Jeni had listened to the night report and wondered how long she could bear to work in a hospital where nothing exciting seemed likely to happen!

In the course of that eight hours she had played an active role in a cardiac arrest and an extubation, and had been suspended from duty for being involved in a missing drug mystery! And now, when she should still have been on duty, she was sitting on the beach, clad in a canary-yellow bikini, with the sun on her back and wavelets breaking gently on the sand a few feet away!

She laughed and dug her toes into the warm sand. Since her conscience was clear and the powers that be knew that she was guilty of nothing more heinous than carelessness with a drug while under pressure of an emergency, she would just enjoy her unexpected holiday and give her mind to nothing more portentous than finishing the sun-tan she had begun last week and planning delicious salads for their boat picnic on Saturday. Perhaps a cake too.

It was a mild, clear day, with just enough wind to have tempted a few sailing boats out through the heads and north to Broken Bay. Further out, a tanker was moving slowly southwards, just beginning to turn in towards the Harbour. The beach was sparsely populated. An elderly couple strolled hand-in-hand along the water's edge. A mother rocked a small child in a pusher and watched another chase a huge coloured ball along the sand. Jeni rolled over on her towel to expose the back of her legs to the sun and rested her head on her folded arms. This was great!

The big beach ball, wildly off course, careened into her. She realised she had been almost asleep. She sat up and patted the ball back to a suddenly subdued small boy whose mother was strongly advising him to be more careful in future.

There was more kick in the sun than she had thought. She reached for the bottle of sun-screen lotion in her beach bag and rubbed a generous amount into her warm shoulders, then twisted her arm behind her, trying to reach the inaccessible area between her shoulderblades.

'Do you need a hand?'

It was the very last voice she had expected to hear here—a deep voice with an unmistakable English accent.

She swung around and looked up. Marc Adams' somewhat apologetic smile acknowledged that she might well be surprised to have him materialise on Manly Beach at this time of day.

'How did you. . .?' She had been going to say, 'know where to find me?' But that would have implied that she thought he had come here especially to see her, and that seemed slightly presumptuous. But why else would he be here, and still wearing the dark trousers, cream silk shirt and blue tie he had had on at work earlier? If he'd come for a casual stroll on the beach he would surely have changed into more suitable gear.

'May I sit down?' he asked.

'Of course.'

She made room for him on her towel and flapped a hand in invitation.

'I guessed I might find you here,' he said. 'I rang

your flat several times and got no answer. I. . .er. . .
I. . .'

Jeni had never seen him at a loss for words before.
He had always been so controlled, so assured.

'Now that I'm here,' he continued, 'I feel rather silly.
About as silly as I look on the beach dressed like this.'

She waved that aside. 'Why *did* you come?' she
asked.

'I was concerned about you. I wanted to make sure
you were all right.'

Their eyes met and held for a long moment before
she looked away, far out to sea where the tanker was
slowly disappearing behind the headland.

'You heard, then?' she said.

'I heard that you'd been suspended. Something to
do with some missing Pethidine.'

She laughed. 'You can't beat a hospital grapevine!'

Because of the concern for her she saw in Marc's
eyes, she wanted to tell him the truth—that her suspension was only temporary and that the people who
mattered did not think she was guilty. But Matron had
insisted that she tell no one. . .

'It's a preposterous accusation!' he snapped. 'I consider Matron's action in suspending you so summarily
to be quite unjustified.'

Jeni had noticed before that when Marc was dis-
turbed about something he tended to use long words
and to enunciate them even more precisely.

'I suppose she did what she had to do,' she said. 'I've
just been resolving not to let myself think about it but
to enjoy all this.' She waved a hand to embrace sea
and sand and sky.

'I'm amazed you can be so philosophical. I had
visions of you being. . .well, quite distressed,' he said.

'And that's why you came?'

'Of course.'

'Thanks.' She picked up a handful of dry sand and let it trickle slowly through her fingers. 'Has it occurred to you that I might be guilty as charged?' she asked quietly.

His head swung round towards her. 'That possibility never crossed my mind.' She could tell by the look of amazement on his face that he spoke the truth.

She lowered her head to hide a sudden rush of tears and had to make an effort to keep her voice steady as she said, 'I'm not guilty. But I'm still a stranger at the hospital. Nobody at the General, where I trained, would have believed for a second that I could have done anything like that.'

'Then remember, they're the ones who matter—the people who know you.'

But you don't know me, she thought. And yet you trust me. And in that moment she saw what they might have had together, if he had not been married. And she felt a rush of fierce envy of the woman who had had much more than his friendship for so many years. How many years? He had said that Sarah was ten. He must have been quite young when she was born. . .conceived. Jeni shut her eyes tightly.

If only. . .! If only he were free! If only she didn't have scruples about his family! But she did, and last night had taught her how vulnerable she was. . .how easily. . .

She opened her hand and let the remainder of the sand fall to the beach. 'How's Mr Burchell?' she asked.

'He's doing all right—breathing quite well, and his colour is good. Pete Stanislav has taken him over again. I did discover, though, before then, that Mr B has a deviated septum which would have been giving him a lot of discomfort and accounted for his agitation and his efforts to remove the tube. Pete looked a bit dumbfounded when I told him about it.'

'He should have discovered it for himself,' said Jeni.

'Quite so. Next time, I guess he'll check.'

It didn't seem at all incongruous to either of them that they should be discussing hospital matters in this situation, because their concern for their patients was never far from their minds.

Marc laughed suddenly and stood up, brushing sand from his trousers. Jeni looked at him questioningly.

'We must look an odd couple,' he explained. 'You in your bikini and I in a suit and tie. I didn't have time to change, and now I must get back for late-afternoon consultations. But first. . .where I came in. . .' He reached out and picked up her bottle of sun lotion. 'Turn round!'

She obeyed, but not before she had bestowed on him a smile which was intended to convey her thanks for his friendship and for his trust in her. In fact, the smile revealed so much more than that that his lips tightened suddenly and he became very absorbed in pouring a small portion of lotion into his hand. And his voice was a trifle unsteady as he said, 'I haven't had a lot of practice at this sort of thing. Sunbathing doesn't rank highly as a national pastime in England. Now, if it was Dencorub. . .!'

His hand was applying the lotion firmly, first to her shoulders, then moving gradually down her back. He began to intone, 'Trapezius, intercostales, spinalis thoracis, latissimus dorsi. . .'

Both his hand and his voice hesitated as he reached the strap of her bikini bra top. When he resumed, the anatomy lesson had ceased, but his touch on her warm skin was a caress, as sensuous as his kiss had been the night before. And, as last night, she didn't want him to stop. . .not ever. She didn't want to have anything to do with her conscience, which was telling her that she must think about the fact that he was married, and not about the wonderful feeling of his hands, so smooth but so disturbing. . .

She swung around, breaking contact with his hand, and knew from the look in his eyes that he had been thinking the same as she had. She took the bottle from his left hand. His right remained suspended in mid-air for several seconds.

Then he lowered it slowly and said lightly, 'I hadn't finished. You'll have a sunburnt spot right over the. . .'

Jeni interrupted before he could elaborate.

'I'll manage. Anyway, it's time I went. Tony said he'd ring me after work, and it must be four o'clock already.'

'Of course! Tony!' Marc's voice was dry.

'We have to finalise arrangements for Saturday. If the weather's like this, it'll be perfect on the water.'

She stood up and took a gaily patterned swatch of material from her bag and wrapped it below her armpits, knotting the ends firmly. She thought she heard him murmur, 'Pity!' but when she looked at him his face was blandly expressionless.

He brushed sand from his clothes again. 'I'll have to find something more suitable than this to wear on Saturday.'

'That might be a good idea,' she agreed. 'And don't forget a hat. Your English complexion won't last five minutes in our sun!'

'It sounds as though I'd better go shopping tomorrow. Care to come along in an advisory capacity?'

Jeni shook her head firmly. 'I'm sure you'll manage.'

'Should I get one of those caps with gold braid?'

She swung round, aghast, then saw the twinkle in his eyes.

'Not that big a boat?' he asked teasingly.

He took her beach-bag in one hand and held her hand with the other, helping her up through the hot dry sand and across the lawn to where his car was parked. She took her bag from him, and as he opened the car door she said, 'I really appreciate your coming down.'

'I'm glad you're coping so well. I'll see you Saturday, then. Can I bring anything?'

'Some wine would be nice. I'm planning to fix some really exotic salads—probably with chicken.'

'Will do. Au revoir.'

He stood and watched as she crossed the street and, as she was walking the short distance to her flat, he drove past and waved. Her step reflected the lightness of her heart.

Back at the flat, Jeni showered and shampooed her hair with the bathroom door open, in case Tony should ring. As she applied conditioner, something niggled at the back of her mind. There was something she had forgotten to do. Then she remembered—not one thing, but two.

She had not told Helen that Mrs Jackson was to be moved into a share room. And she had not gone back to talk to Mrs Petersen and try and find out what was worrying her about her discharge.

Helen would be off duty by now, but she must ring in, anyway. She rinsed her hair, dried herself quickly and pulled on a white terry towelling gown. She twisted a towel around her wet hair and dialled the hospital number. The voice that purred, 'Women's Surgical,' when Switchboard put her through was unfamiliar.

'Jeni Tremaine speaking. Is Sister there, please?'

'This is Sister. Who did you say is calling?'

'Jeni Tremaine. I'm on the staff of the unit.'

There was a not very subtle change in the tone of the voice at the other end of the line. The purr was gone and the vowel sounds were distinctly less rounded.

'Oh, you mean you *were* on the staff. I understand you've been suspended over a drug matter.'

Jeni kept the anger that surged in her under control, but there was a cutting edge to her voice as she said, 'I *have* been suspended, but that doesn't mean I'm guilty. Or has assumption of guilt replaced assumption of innocence?'

'Where there's smoke there's usually fire,' said the voice. 'What was the purpose of your call?'

'There are two matters I should have reported before I left this morning,' said Jeni. 'Firstly, Dr Adams thinks Mrs Jackson would be better in a share room, and Mrs Jackson has agreed to try sharing.'

'That's already been taken care of. Mrs Jackson couldn't understand why nothing had been said, so she mentioned it herself. Dr Adams has also been back to the ward.'

'Oh, good! Who's she sharing with?' asked Jeni.

'I don't think that need concern you now. What was the other thing you had to report?'

Jeni took a deep breath. She had known this sort of reaction was possible, but was not really prepared for it. But Marc's words, that it was the people who knew and trusted her who mattered, popped into her mind and she was able to say, with reasonable equanimity, 'Mrs Petersen didn't seem happy about going home tomorrow. I thought perhaps somebody should talk to her and find out what's bothering her.'

'May I suggest that you leave the running of the ward to those of us who are still employed here?'

'I'll do that—with the greatest of pleasure!' And Jeni slammed the receiver down.

She was still standing there, fuming, when it rang again. She answered abruptly.

'Jeni Tremaine!'

'Hi,' said Tony. 'What's up? You sound. . .' He hesitated.

'Try "infuriated"—"ready to kill"!' Jeni snapped.

'Who? Me?' He seemed really worried.

'Of course not. Why would I be angry with you?'

'Just checking! So what *is* the cause of this very atypical outburst?'

'It's a long story that you don't have time to listen to now. I'll fill you in on Saturday—perhaps I'll have calmed down by then!'

'I'll look forward to it—I think! About Saturday—there'll be a couple of extras.'

'I'd have been surprised if there hadn't been.' Tony being Tony, there could have been a half a dozen ringins by now. There still could be, by Saturday. 'Who are they?' she asked.

'Charlene and James.'

She laughed. 'Now there's an unlikely pair!'

James was one of Tony's fellow RMOs, a nice person and excellent doctor, but so wrapped up in his profession as to appear incapable of seeing even a sexy blonde bombshell like Charlene as anything more than an interesting conjunction of anatomical parts.

Tony chuckled too. 'I agree with you—the cerebral and the physical. Actually, *I* asked James, and *Liz* invited Charlene, quite independently.'

'Is Liz staying here Friday night?'

'Apparently not. She asked me for a lift to the marina on Saturday morning.'

'Oh.' Jeni's disappointment sounded in her voice.

'I'm beginning to feel lonesome here on my own. I've seen so little of anyone since I've been back.'

'Pressure of work, I guess, honey—you know how it is. The girls said not to worry about lunch. We'll pick something up on the day.'

'Tell them not to bother,' said Jeni. 'I've got a couple of extra days off and will have plenty of time to fix lunch.'

'Extra days? How come? No, I'd better not stop now. We'll see you at nine-thirty at the marina. Will you see that Marc knows where to go?'

'Right! Bye. Don't work too hard.'

'Bye, honey.'

Jeni replaced the receiver thoughtfully. Two more days without seeing any of the old crowd. She would have been glad to talk over the events of today with someone who understood and who was not associated with the hospital and therefore not under Matron's embargo. But that would have to wait till Saturday.

CHAPTER SIX

SATURDAY was a perfect day for sailing. The sun shone from a blue sky which had just the right sprinkling of white, scudding clouds. The ten- to fifteen-knot wind could have been made to a sailor's orders.

Jeni had spent Friday shopping and chopping and mixing, and was feeling very satisfied with the assortment of salads in Tupperware containers which she loaded out of the refrigerator into a king-size Esky. She had made a large quiche and bought two barbecued chickens and some fresh king prawns. There were several kinds of fresh fruit, including some kiwi fruit and a large mango which she thought Marc might find interesting. A big fruit cake was already cut into generous-sized slabs.

Marc had rung earlier that morning and insisted on picking her up at her flat. He arrived on time, looking somewhat self-conscious about his attire, which consisted of a red and white polo shirt, white cotton beach pants and a pair of yellow boat shoes.

'Well? Do I pass muster?' he asked, aware of her quick appraisal.

She nodded. 'Very nautical! I couldn't have chosen better myself. Some of it looks a trifle new, but that won't last long, especially if you treat it as you're treating that hat.'

He laughed and relaxed his grip on the soft broad-brimmed hat clutched in his right hand.

'You look very nice yourself.'

The comment was banal enough, but there was

nothing banal about the warmth of his voice and the approval in his eyes.

Jeni's open, oversized yellow shirt revealed a black and white one-piece swimsuit under white shorts. Her boat shoes were white.

Marc picked up the Esky in one hand and her picnic basket in the other and raised his eyebrows.

'Are we feeding the five thousand?' he queried.

'No. Just five Aussies and one Englishman who'll all build up quite an appetite out on the water. And one never knows when Tony will have invited several more. It pays to be prepared.'

They chatted about nothing very much during the ten minutes it took Marc to drive from Manly to Clontarf, where Tony's boat, *Rheya*, was berthed, just to the south-east of the Spit Bridge on Middle Harbour. Jeni explained to Marc that Middle Harbour was a long arm of Sydney Harbour, off to the north.

They were the last to arrive. Tony and James were already on the boat, checking the shrouds and stays and pulling off the hatch covers to air the boat before getting under way.

'G'day, you two,' shouted Tony. It was clear he was looking forward to a day on the water. 'Give us a minute and we'll come over to the dock—it'll save rowing across and picking you up in the dinghy.'

Liz and Charlene, who had been bent over the boot of Tony's car, straightened up at the sound of Tony's voice and, seeing Jeni and Marc, came across to them.

Charlene's eyes widened slightly when she saw Marc, and Jeni was amused to see how vivaciously she responded to her introduction to him. Charlene was nothing if not predictable where men were concerned. Jeni wondered whether she should drop a casual remark, now, about Marc's wife and family, but decided it would be too obvious a ruse. Perhaps later. . .

Charlene was wearing white shorts and a pink cotton top which did all the right things for her curvaceous figure. She too had on a wide-brimmed hat, like Marc's, to protect her fair skin from the sun. Liz's red maillot was almost completely covered by a huge, floppy white windcheater. Her legs were bare, long and slim and beautifully tanned, as though she had been spending a lot of time in the sun recently.

Soon Tony and James brought the boat over to the dock. Marc was introduced to James, the picnic gear was stowed away, and everyone climbed aboard. Apart from a slight consciousness of Marc as a new member of their group, they all seemed relaxed and happy.

Tony, who was the authority about winds and tides, suggested they sail up Middle Harbour to Bantry Bay. This meant that they had to wait for the Spit Bridge to open, which it was scheduled to do at ten o'clock. The waiting time was spent explaining some of the mysteries of sailing to Marc and answering the one or two intelligent questions he asked.

Then it was time to go through the Bridge, which they did under motor power. Once through, Tony quickly stopped the motor, and they had the mainsail and a number two Genoa up and set in a matter of minutes.

'How long to Bantry Bay, Cap'n?' someone asked.

Tony considered. 'On a day like this, the winds in Middle Harbour can be flukey. It might take one and a half hours, but don't hold me to that.'

'It sounds as though we should do it comfortably by lunchtime,' said Jeni.

'Are you planning to swim somewhere? I haven't got a costume with me,' said Marc.

'Not to worry. We shan't be swimming at Bantry Bay—too risky.'

'Currents?'

'Sharks!'

'Oh!'

James took Marc below and they brought cushions up from the bunks and spread them around the cockpit. Charlene and Liz disappeared and emerged a little later with huge, half-filled mugs of coffee and a plate of fruit cake. Jeni was told she was exempt from cabin duty for the day, as she had provided the food.

They sat admiring the magnificent waterfront homes they were passing, and listening to the flap of the sails overhead and the slapping of the water on the sides of the boat. When the breeze died down momentarily, the sun was warm and soothing—soporific almost, to minds and bodies recently released from the demands and responsibilities of hospital work.

Every ingredient for a perfect day was there. But, before long, Jeni sensed that restraints and undercurrents were developing. Even Tony—especially Tony, she realised with surprise—was not his usual happy-go-lucky self. Usually, when he was on the water, nothing bothered him. But now he seemed subdued and restrained, as though something was upsetting him.

James too was quiet, but that was not unusual. When he had that remote look, as though he was turning Einstein's theory of relativity over in his mind, his friends simply let him alone until he chose to join the human race again. When he did so, he could be the life of the party.

Charlene was behaving true to form, given the presence of a handsome new male in their midst. Marc would have had to be pretty thick, Jeni thought, not to be aware of Charlene's wiles, but he was being polite and pleasant to her, as he was to everyone else. With one exception, Jeni realised, and had to repress a sudden surge of jealousy. Liz was getting more than her fair share of Marc's attention. He sat next to her when lunch was served; he engaged her in a long conversation at the other end of the boat. Jeni could overhear enough to know that much of their conversation was hospital talk. But she also heard him ask Liz several personal questions, such as he had never bothered to ask Jeni.

Tony, as usual, was absorbed in sailing the boat. But whereas usually she would have been working happily alongside him, today he seemed not to want her there. Once, when she was on the jib sheets, he rebuked her sharply for a sloppy tack. And that was not like Tony at all.

Feeling confused and despondent, she went and sat on the bow, dangling her legs through the rails, as soon as she was released from her chore. She tried to convince herself that it was the change in Tony's attitude that was making her feel so miserable, but eventually she had to admit that Marc's obvious attraction to Liz far outweighed Tony's change of attitude towards herself.

The tension was broken somewhat when, just as they were passing Castlecrag, *Rheya* was hit by an eighteen to twenty-knot bullet of wind which heeled her hard over and sent coffee-cups flying around the cockpit. Fortunately most of them were empty. Tony, on the helm, came in for some goodnatured abuse from the others for not having anticipated the sudden wind shift.

After that, everyone seemed more relaxed and comfortable with one another. They ate their lunch on the boat, tied up to one of the old deserted munitions stores that ringed the shore at Bantry Bay.

There were oohs and aahs over Jeni's salads. Charlene asked, 'Whenever did you have time to do all this, Jeni?'

'Oh, I've had a couple of extra days off,' Jeni explained.

Everyone, except Marc, looked surprised.

'How come?' they asked.

Jeni caught Marc's eye and a small gleam of amusement passed between them as they anticipated the response of the others to her explanation. But also in Marc's eyes was concern as to how she would handle the revelation she was about to make.

'I've been suspended,' she told them.

'You've *what*?' Four pairs of eyes fastened on her in amazement.

She laughed. 'You all look as if the doctor has just told you to say "aah"!'

Four mouths were promptly closed, then came a clamour of voices.

'You're kidding, right?'

'Whatever for?'

Jeni stole another glance at Marc before she said, as though it was something that happened every day of the week to her, 'On suspicion of stealing drugs.'

This time they were too stunned to say anything for a time, but sat staring at her.

Then, 'They're crazy!'

'You? Never in a thousand years!'

Marc was looking at her with a smile in his eyes and, when he nodded his head ever so slightly, she could hear him saying, again, 'These are the people who matter—the ones who know you.'

They were all clamouring for explanations. If it had not been for Marc's presence, she might have told them the whole story. As it was, she told them as much as she could.

'And you were suspended—just like that—without there being a scrap of evidence against you?'

This was James speaking and, as usual, when he gave utterance, they all listened.

'You know, Jeni,' he continued thoughtfully, 'you might have cause for litigation against the hospital over this.'

'Good idea. Go for it, girl!'

They all agreed with James. Tony added vehemently, 'I'll appear as a character witness for you. And I might have a few extra things to say, too, about a hospital that treats its staff as shabbily as that.'

'Thanks,' smiled Jeni, 'But I don't think it will come to that.'

The talk went on. There were no undercurrents now. They were united in a common cause, rallying loyally to her support. Jeni felt bad that she could not tell them the whole story, but she promised herself she would do so just as soon as she possibly could.

'So that's why you sounded so upset when I rang the other day,' said Tony.

'Yes.' She gave a brief account of the conversation she had had with the ward sister. Marc had something to add to that.

'I saw that particular sister earlier that afternoon,' he said. 'We talked about shifting Mrs Jackson into a share room. Sister Coulter managed to get in a snide word or two about you and drugs. I'm afraid I rather put her in her place and came down heavily in your defence. You probably got the backlash of our conversation when you rang.'

There was a murmur of approval which indicated that Marc's stock had just risen considerably with those present. Jeni felt a thrill of gratitude that he should have done that for her.

'Do you know how the rest of the staff have reacted?' she asked.

'I haven't heard much—I still only have three or four patients in the hospital. But I would say it's a fairly mixed reaction.'

She nodded. That was predictable.

Marc continued. 'You'll be surprised when I tell you who's been your most vocal supporter.'

She looked at him enquiringly. 'Who?'

'Mrs Jackson.'

'Truly? I find that hard to believe.'

'Nevertheless! She won't hear a word against you— almost refused to let anyone else nurse her for a time. I think she thought that by going on strike she could force them to recall you.'

'Mrs Jackson of all people!' Jeni shook her head. 'Patients never cease to amaze me.'

They all joined in, then, with anecdotes about the unpredictable, unexpected things that patients had said or done. All except Marc, who had suddenly become very quiet.

Everyone seemed a little more relaxed after lunch, when they turned about and headed for home. But Tony's mood soon deteriorated again. Not only that, but Jeni became convinced that something she had suspected ever since returning from England was true—Liz and Charlene did not seem to want to accept her back on their former friendly sharing basis. They were restrained in her presence, slightly uncomfortable, as though they were having to watch what they said in case. . . In case what?

She shook her head. Something was badly out of sync with them all, somehow, but she had no idea what it was or what could be done about it. She went and sat once more on the bow, and this time James joined her there, not saying much, but seeming to know how she was feeling. She was glad of his company. It was better than being alone.

James, nice man that he was, probably thought she was upset about Tony's unusual behaviour towards her. She could not tell him the truth. She could hardly even admit it to herself—that it was Marc's continued attention to Liz which was the cause of her low spirits.

One could not blame Marc either. Liz was one of those people who looked beautiful in any clothes, at any time. She had discarded her windcheater now, and was wearing only her red swimsuit. Her black hair was tousled by the wind and her eyes were bright. She, anyway, appeared to be enjoying to the full their day's sailing. Or was it Marc's seeming attraction to her that gave rise to the small smile of contentment that had played around her lips most of the day?

Jeni wished suddenly that the day was over and she were home alone in her flat. Then she was ashamed of the thought, and had just decided to make a determined effort to cast her woes aside and be cheerful, when she became aware that Marc was talking to Tony now. The wind was blowing most of their words away from her, but, as it dropped momentarily, she heard Tony ask, 'When do they arrive in Australia, then?'

'I'm not quite sure. I'm expecting to hear any time,' Marc replied.

Jeni missed Tony's next remark, but she heard Marc say, 'Not yet. I know I've left it rather late. I hope I can find an apartment for them for the time being.'

He was obviously talking about his family. But why did he say, 'for them' and not, 'for us'?

James, unaware that Jeni was hanging on every word

of the conversation going on behind them, said something, and again she missed Tony's next comment. But she heard Marc's reply.

'It is a responsibility, yes. But I promised Paul I'd do all I could for them. And I *have* become very fond of them.'

Jeni could make nothing of this. But, even as she groped to understand what lay behind Marc's words, a small flicker of something like hope was born within her. Tony's next words fanned the flicker into a flame. He said, 'It seems to me you've taken on a lot of the responsibilities of a married man, without the advantages.'

Marc made a non-committal, enigmatic sort of response, and the conversation lapsed. A moment or two later Tony announced that they had made such good time back that he thought they could manage a swim at Balmoral, where it was safe from sharks. He called to James to take over the boat while he went below to fossick out a pair of old swimming trunks for Marc to wear.

Jeni was left alone, frantically trying to fit what she had just heard into her preconceived ideas about Marc Adams. But she was not being very successful, because she was experiencing a sense of relief and of almost delirious happiness that made coherent thinking difficult.

One thing was clear. He was not married!

She had seen him with a family and had jumped to the conclusion that it was his family. She had seen him with a woman and had assumed that she was his wife.

And she had been wrong!

She had thought it strange that he had been so reluctant to talk about his family. But they were not his family. He must have assumed, when they went looking at schools together, that she knew that, or surely he would have explained.

And when she had rejected him that night in her flat, he had thought it was because of Tony, and she, thinking him to be married, had encouraged him to believe that.

So there was no reason on earth why he should not have paid attention to Liz today. He was not being disloyal to a wife in England, or to herself, or to anyone at all. He was free to pay attention to anyone he chose.

Liz? How much did she actually have to fear from Liz? Marc had met Liz for only the second time today. He might be attracted to her—what man wouldn't be?—but things could not have progressed very far in that time. Anyway, Jeni thought, all's fair in love and war. She would have no compunction about entering the lists against Liz.

If only she had known Marc was not married that night in the flat, when he had kissed her. Reliving those moments and what they might have led to, had she not pushed him away, she wished they were alone now, so that she could go to him and explain, feel his arms around her, experience his kisses.

But that would be too humiliating if he had, in the meantime, fallen for Liz. Also, Jeni remembered, she had some unfinished business with Tony, which should be cleared up before much longer. Tony's attitude towards her since her return from England and his behaviour today convinced Jeni that he would be just as willing as she was to formally end their relationship. And then. . .

Life had suddenly become a whole new ball-game. And the referee seemed to be on her side for a change.

CHAPTER SEVEN

THEY anchored *Rheya* in a little cove near Balmoral Bay for their swim.

Tony seemed to have shed his gremlins. He and Jeni, who were stronger swimmers than the others, dived and swam and raced one another, just as they had always done.

Several times Jeni was aware of Marc watching them, but he stayed close to Liz. James was with Charlene, whose swimming ability amounted to treading water, splashing and squealing. There were other people in the water, mostly between the group from *Rheya* and the shore.

Jeni and Tony had converged on James and Charlene, and Tony became involved in the swimming lesson James was giving Charlene. Jeni turned and swam off in the direction of Marc and Liz, with some half-formed thought in her mind that the sooner she began her campaign to cut short any developing relationship between Marc and Liz the better. She was still a little distance from them when she heard Marc give a warning shout and saw him plunge through the water away from Liz. He was swimming with strong, clean strokes towards a tall youth who was standing stock-still, gazing down into the water with a look of horror on his face. It was only when a form—a female form in a red swimsuit—broke the surface of the water, floating face downward, that Jeni had any idea of what had happened. Then she too changed direction.

She and Marc were about equidistant from the

floating form and, with all the strength she could muster, she cut through the sea. Again she heard Marc shout, and caught his words of warning to the youth— 'Don't touch her!'

A few seconds later he and Jeni were both at the scene and Marc was again ordering the youth to, 'Stand back and don't do a thing!' The youth looked unsure whether to obey or not, until Marc said brusquely, 'I'm a doctor.'

Jeni looked at Marc, seeking some information about what had happened. He said shortly, 'She dived off his shoulders. Went in too straight—water's too shallow.'

The water was indeed barely up to his armpits when he stood erect, and Jeni was just able to touch bottom and steady herself. Several other swimmers, hearing Marc's shouts, had approached and were watching from a little distance. Marc called out in their direction, 'Get an ambulance! Tell them probable spinal injury.'

Two people began swimming and then splashing their way to shore. Jeni, thinking ahead swiftly, looked round and saw a man with a surfboard under his arm. She beckoned him and asked, 'Can we have that, please?'

Marc, having positioned himself at the unconscious girl's head but being careful not to touch it, was pushing one of her arms down along her side. Then, with one hand on her spine and the other beneath her other armpit, he gently turned her over so that she was face up in the water.

With the girl on her back, both of Marc's hands were immobilised, one supporting her spine, the other, with fingers spreadeagled, beneath her head. Quickly Jeni moved in and placed a careful finger on her neck.

'There's a pulse,' she said.

'Good! Breathing?'

'No. But there's a surfboard. . .'

'Great. Slide it under.'

As Jeni tipped the end of the board to submerge it below the girl, Tony moved in on the other side and, keeping the board level, they allowed it to float upwards, centring it as exactly as they could beneath the girl's spine. At that precise moment, Marc slid his hands out from under her and allowed the board to take her weight.

Instantly, as if they had rehearsed the whole procedure many times before, James and Liz were there too, James beside Jeni, Liz beside Tony, holding the board steady and level.

Thank goodness the sea is calm, thought Jeni. To have had to deal with a spine-injured victim in a choppy or rough sea would have made the outcome very much less favourable.

As his four offsiders supported the board strongly, Marc lifted the girl's chin and began mouth-to-mouth resuscitation. Fortunately it was not long before her chest gave a heave. There was a gurgling sound in her throat and then she was taking regular if shallow breaths. The sigh of relief from her rescuers was audible to the small crowd of onlookers, and a murmur of approval came from them.

Jeni had been too absorbed to notice, until now, that one of the onlookers was wearing the distinctive cap of a surf lifesaver. He pressed forward with them as the team began moving the surfboard and its occupant slowly towards the shore, but he did not attempt to intervene, merely saying, 'An ambulance is on the beach.'

Ten minutes later the girl, wrapped in blankets, was in the ambulance, together with her still shocked boyfriend, and it was moving slowly across the firm wet sand towards the road, as the crowd of onlookers dispersed in all directions.

The six rescuers stood and looked at one another.

'Good job, Marc!' said Tony.

'Jeni too,' added James.

'I hope she's not too badly injured,' said Marc.

'It would have been a lot worse if you'd not been there. If anyone had tried to drag her from the water. . .' They all winced.

'Hope we hear how she gets on. Anyone get her name?'

'No. But the ambulance officer took mine,' said Marc.

'Let's know if you get news of her.'

'Will do.'

The whole episode had taken less than twenty minutes, about as long as it took for the group to return to *Rheya* and get her under way again. Back at Clontarf, they packed the sails away and gave the boat a quick wash-down. Then the same sense of awkwardness that had been evident at times during the day descended again.

Jeni had expected that everyone would go back to her flat for showers and a snack and a relaxed evening. That was what would have happened in days gone by. But Liz seemed impatient to get back to the hospital, making a vague reference to an engagement. Marc immediately offered to drive her, but Tony quickly said he had to go back anyway to check up on a patient. James asked if they could drop him at his parents' home in Mosman on the way, and Charlene looked hopefully at Marc, but when no invitation from him was forthcoming, she reluctantly said she'd better go to the hospital too, as she was on duty in the morning.

They all piled into Tony's car and drove off, leaving

Marc and Jeni standing in a somewhat strained silence.
Marc stowed the picnic gear into the back of the car
and said very little on the drive back to Manly. Jeni
suspected his thoughts were following Liz and regret-
ting that his evening had not turned out as he had
apparently hoped.

At the flat, he helped Jeni upstairs with her baggage
but refused her offer of a drink. Before he went, he
took her hands in both of his and asked anxiously, as
though he had some doubts but really cared, whether
she had enjoyed her day.

She laughed a little uncertainly.

'It was quite a day. I guess you could say it had
plenty of everything. And yes, in some ways it
was. . .rather special.'

He didn't ask her to elaborate, but said, 'I'm glad.'

And was gone.

Jeni faced her return to duty on Monday with mixed
feelings. Traffic had delayed her and the members of
the afternoon shift were already gathered in the duty-
room, waiting for Helen to hand over to them. Every
face turned towards Jeni with varying degrees of
interest and speculation when she walked in. Helen's
perfectly normal greeting restored Jeni's fragile
equilibrium.

'Nice to have you back, Jeni. Good days off?'

'Lovely, thanks.'

'Now, let's see. Kate you know, but I don't think
you've met Jane or Annette.'

Kate and Annette were nurses. Jane was sister in
charge that afternoon. She looked at Jeni with curios-
ity, but when she smiled and said, 'Hello' Jeni knew,
to her relief, that this was not the person she had
spoken to on the phone, the day she was suspended.

Helen said, 'We've been discharging and admitting patients ever since you went off, Jeni. And the surgeons have been at it again this morning. So you'll all have a busy time.'

She was right. Jeni's list consisted of three post-anaesthetic patients, as well as several convalescent ones. Time flew as she checked drips, took blood pressures, pulses, sponged and sat up patients, made sure they did breathing and coughing exercises. She revelled in it. Several times during the morning, the realisation that Marc was not, after all, married lent wings to her feet. Once or twice she remembered that she was still under a cloud as far as the other staff members were concerned, but the thought did not have the power to daunt her. Nothing had the power to daunt her today.

When she went into Mrs Jackson's room she found her holding court in a room full of visitors and flowers, dressed in a frilly pink gown, her hair piled high and her face lavishly made up. Once again her universe was revolving about her, and she was loving every minute.

'Mrs Jackson! I almost didn't recognise you. You look fantastic,' said Jeni, and, seeing Mrs Jackson about to introduce her to her visitors, added hastily, 'I'm very busy. I'll see you later,' and retreated thankfully.

She was checking the blood-pressure of a thirteen-year-old girl called Patti, who had had an emergency appendicectomy the night before, when Marc walked in and stood on the opposite side of the bed.

'Carry on, Sister,' he said.

Patti was pert and pretty and seemingly quite unself-conscious about the bands on her teeth. She gazed at Marc with wide-eyed adulation.

'Isn't he just the *most*?' she asked with a rapturous sigh.

Jeni avoided catching Marc's eye, in case he read in hers the fact that she thoroughly agreed with Patti's assessment. She concentrated on rolling up the sphygmomanometer cuff, saying lightly, and with the merest edge to her voice, 'He's also probably very used to having female patients fall madly in love with him. It's an occupational hazard for doctors, you know, Patti.'

Now she did glance up at him, and was surprised to see him flush slightly and his lips tighten, as though he had been offended by her comment. But he was still smiling as he looked down at Patti.

'Cut the blarney, young lady, and let me look at those stitches.'

Patti sighed, as though his suggestion were the height of bliss. She threw back the bedclothes and pulled up her shortie nightgown, revealing the briefest of bright pink bikini panties.

Marc gently and briefly palpated the area around the plaster covering the wound low down on Patti's right side.

'That's fine,' he said, and replaced the bedclothes firmly. 'No problems, Sister?'

'No, Doctor, everything is normal.'

'Then I'll see you tomorrow, Patti. You can probably go home the day after that.'

Patti's face fell. 'Do I have to?' she asked.

'The hospital is very short of beds just now,' he explained to her. 'And anyway,' he added, teasingly, 'patients don't usually complain about being discharged.'

'Will you come and see me at home, then?'

He chuckled at the lovelorn expression she assumed.

'No. But, if you're very good, you can come and see me in my rooms and I'll take your stitches out.'

'Oh, good!' she beamed.

Marc looked at Jeni and laughed, shrugging his shoulders expressively.

'May I see you outside for a moment, Sister?'

She nodded. He said goodbye to Patti and followed Jeni from the room, carefully closing the door behind him.

'I suddenly feel very old!' he grinned. 'Thirteen years! Are all Aussie youngsters so precocious at that age?'

Jeni would happily have stayed talking with him about the idiosyncrasies of Australian children, or about anything else for that matter, but she had other patients she should see. He saw her glance down at the fob watch hanging on her uniform, and said, 'I won't delay you. I just wanted to find out how things are for you, back at work.'

'I've been so busy I haven't had time to think about anything but patients,' she replied.

'Good! Let me know if things get tough and I can be of help at all.'

'Thanks. I'm sure I'll manage.'

His eyes lingered on her face for a moment. 'And of course you have. . .your friends, if you need support.'

The gentleness was gone from his voice now, and abruptly, he turned and walked away. Jeni had a momentary impulse to call him back and tell him there was no one she would rather go to for help, if she needed it, than him. But she had determined to do nothing like that until she had finalised things with Tony. And, too, there was Liz.

She resolutely turned her mind to her next patient,

and sped off along the corridor in the opposite direction to Marc Adams.

The day continued to fly. When it was time to report off duty, she told the rest of the shift not to wait for her as she had an intravenous drip which was nearly through and she wanted to change it over before she left. By the time she had hung up the new vacolitre and gone to the duty-room to chart it, the others had gone.

Harry Scott, the night sister whom she had met one day last week, was sitting at the table with the report book open in front of him and his long, white-clad legs stretched out halfway across the room. He drew them in as Jeni walked over to the case-note trolley.

She said, 'Hi!'

'Hi! Have we met?'

'Not really, I guess. I was here one morning last week when you were handing over. It was only my second day at the hospital. I've been off for four days since then.'

'Oh!'

He did not say, 'Yes, I remember,' but she saw a dawning realisation in his eyes and knew he had just worked out who she was. There was nothing in his voice or his manner to indicate how he felt about nurses who purloined drugs, and when he did not say anything further she asked, as she extracted a file from the trolley, 'Are you on permanent nights?'

'Yes—Monday through Thursday, relieving. I do two nights here and two in Men's Surgical.' He jerked a thumb at the floor. 'And what about you?'

'This is my first appointment since I finished training. It may be short-lived, at that.'

He made an exclamation of some sort. It was not a question—he was not asking her to explain what she meant. Jeni popped the file back in its place in the trolley and turned towards him. He was looking at her rather intently, but, as their glances met, he wiped some unreadable expression from his face and said lightly, 'Lovely tan you have.'

'Yes. We were out on the boat on Saturday.'

This time she *could* read his expression. He was interested and enthusiastic.

'You have a boat?'

'My friends do,' she told him. 'We often go out. Or we used to.'

'*Used* to?' he queried.

'I've been overseas for three months. Since I came back, everything's changed. . .' She couldn't prevent a small catch in her voice and turned away for a moment. When she looked back at Harry he was watching her, and she felt he was seeing more than she had had any intention of revealing. Last week, hearing him read his report, she had been impressed by his empathy for his patients. Now she knew that same empathy was being directed towards herself. He would be very easy to talk to, for the simple reason that he saw her as a person with feelings and problems and not just a pretty face and certain physical attributes—which was about as far as most men would have got at this stage of an acquaintanceship.

But she should have been off duty some time ago and he had a busy night ahead of him.

She restored the chart she was holding to its place and said, 'I must go. It's been nice talking to you. Have a good night.'

He pulled his long frame out of the chair and stood up.

'Yes,' he said. 'Be seeing you around.'

'Goodnight.'

* * *

Jeni decided to leave her car at home next morning. She had found she could go by hydrofoil ferry to Circular Quay and then back across the Harbour to Cremorne Point in much the same time as it took her to drive through morning peak-hour traffic to the hospital. And it was so much more relaxing than driving. She sat outside on the ferry, facing into the wind and breathing deeply of the sea air.

She was earlier than usual arriving at the hospital and, even though she spent several minutes in the staff-room, combing the tangles out of her hair, she was still the first of the day staff to arrive in the duty-room.

Harry was there alone, just sitting gazing at the report book open in front of him. He looked tired and subdued, but that was not unusual for night staff, after a heavy night. Jeni smiled at him and said, 'Hello again! Have you had a busy night?'

'Busy enough, but straightforward.'

A voice behind her said, 'Good morning, Harry.'

Jeni recognised the voice immediately as being the one she had heard on the phone last week.

She turned around slowly. The owner of the voice was a short, rather plump woman in her mid-thirties. She had fine, brown hair, which had been expertly— and expensively, Jeni assessed—cut and shaped. Her make-up, too, had been well executed, and Jeni thought her face would have been attractive, in spite of its plainness, if her expression had been more pleasant. She was looking at Jeni as if she were quite beneath contempt.

'I am Sister Coulter. And you must be Sister Tremaine,' she said, in a voice which left no one in any doubt about how she felt about nurses who meddled with drugs.

'Yes,' said Jeni.

'I'm surprised to see you back on duty, I must say.'

'I'm here at Matron's request,' Jeni said quietly.

'I know that. But let's get things straight. While I'm in charge of the ward and responsible for what happens in it, you will not handle any drugs whatsoever. If any of your patients need medication, you will come to me and I will administer it. Is that understood?'

As Sister spoke, she had moved to sit down at the other end of the table from Harry, and Jeni, turning to face her, became aware that Harry was watching the scene with absorbed interest. She gave him the merest glimmer of a smile, to reassure him that she was not unduly cowed by Sister's remarks. Then, standing up straight and clasping her hands behind her back, she said, in mock parody of a student nurse on the mat, 'Yes, Sister.'

Harry's lips twitched and Sister looked back at Jeni suspiciously. But the two nurses walked in at that moment and nothing more was said.

Harry read his report, but he seemed abstracted, and there were none of the humorous comments and anecdotes Jeni remembered from the last time she had heard him hand over.

In the mild hubbub that broke out in the duty-room after the report was finished, and before the girls went off to start their work, Harry managed to lay a hand briefly on Jeni's arm and murmur, 'Don't worry about *her*. Everything will be all right.'

It was nice of him to say so, and she smiled her thanks before going off to gather up her bundle of linen for her first bed-make.

The spate of surgical cases was continuing this morning, and Jeni had two patients to prepare for theatre, as well as her quota of other patients. She had no respite until her breakfast break at eight-thirty.

After the break, she went straight to the flower-room and was deftly removing wilted blooms from the bottom of long stems of gladioli when Sister Coulter came to the door.

'Matron wants to see you in her office,' she said, with a note of snide complacency in her voice. She continued to stand there, watching, perhaps expecting to see Jeni wilt like the blooms she was handling. Jeni quietly replaced two more stems in the bowl and topped it up with water from a large jug.

'Mrs Brown's pre-med is due at nine,' she said. 'I presume you'll see to it, whether or not I'm back by then?'

'Of course!'

Matron was sitting behind her table, her hands clasped in front of her, doing nothing and looking quite bemused, when Jeni knocked and went in.

'Good morning, Jeni. Sit down.'

Before Jeni had time to comply, Matron went on.

'The most extraordinary thing has happened—it's really quite amazing!'

Jeni raised her eyebrows expectantly, and Matron wasted no words in getting to the heart of what she had to say.

'Harry Scott came to see me a little while ago, just after I arrived on duty, and confessed to having pur-loined drugs on several occasions.'

'Harry? Oh, no!'

'That was my reaction too—dismay and disbelief. He's been working here for twelve months and has been one of our best nurses. Frankly, I've become quite fond of him.' Matron shook her head slowly from side to side.

Jeni said, 'I've only met him three times, on duty, but I can understand how you feel. He's so very. . .'

she searched for the right word '. . .likeable. But why did he do it? Surely he doesn't have a drug habit?'

'Not really. He apparently had knee surgery just before coming here, and occasionally has a need for analgesics. He could easily have got a prescription for something, but it seems there was some sort of challenge—devilment, perhaps—in helping himself—to prove it could be done without anyone being any the wiser,' Matron explained.

'But nobody *was* any the wiser—at least, not that it was he who was taking them. He could just have stopped, said nothing, and that would have been the end of it. Why did he come to you and confess?'

'Because, being the nice person he is, apparently he couldn't bear to see you being blamed for what he'd done. I think he would have owned up, whoever it was that was under suspicion. But you seem to have made a particular impression on him. And then this morning, he told me, one of the staff was quite unpleasant to you about it, in his presence, and that finally decided him to make a clean breast of it.'

Jeni drew a deep sigh. 'I'm sorry. I'm really sorry.'

'So am I,' said Matron. Then she laughed wryly. 'Here we are lamenting, when we should be rejoicing! In the long run it will be a good thing for Harry too. He's promised me that, if he needs it, he'll have therapy, but I don't think his habit is that bad. And I'm sure he won't try any more such capers. In fact,' Matron looked a little abashed, 'I've done something quite irregular under the circumstances. I told him I'd give him a reference! He didn't ask for one—if he had I probably would have refused. But he really is an excellent nurse and it would be a waste if he couldn't continue in the profession.'

Jeni nodded in agreement. 'I'm glad,' she said, then added thoughtfully, 'So that's the end of that.'

'Not quite the end,' Matron said. 'Our scheming has paid off, because, if you hadn't agreed to play along, we might never have known who the culprit was. We're grateful to you, Jeni, and I'll make sure that the whole hospital knows that you were never really under suspicion.'

She pressed a button on her desk and, almost immediately a secretary appeared with some papers in her hand. She handed them to Matron, gave Jeni a friendly smile, and departed.

Matron read the top page through before handing it to Jeni. 'I think that covers it,' she said.

The staff of the hospital are hereby informed that our recent problem involving missing drugs has been resolved to our complete satisfaction. We wish to express our thanks to Sister Jeni Tremaine for the role she played, at no small personal cost, in helping us to identify the person responsible. At no time was she herself under suspicion.

When Jeni finished reading and looked up, Matron said, 'I have just one more request. Would you feel happy about us not revealing the name of the person who was responsible?'

'Oh, yes!' Jeni said fervently.

'People might, of course, put two and two together when Harry doesn't reappear, but, as he's relieving night staff, his absence may not be noticed until the dust has settled.'

'I hope so.'

Jeni held the paper in her hand out towards Matron. But Matron shook her head.

'I'm having a copy of that posted in the staff dining-room where everyone will see it. I would like you, personally, to hand the one you have to Sister Coulter and ask her, as from me, to pin it on the noticeboard in your ward.'

There was a mischievous gleam in Matron's eyes as she continued, 'That's what one might call, in a small way, retributive justice.'

Jeni grinned back at her. 'I'll be happy to do that, Matron. And thank you.'

'Thank *you*, Jeni, once again.'

Sister Coulter was sitting alone in the duty-room, writing, when Jeni entered. She looked up as Jeni handed her the paper and said quietly, 'Matron has asked that you pin this on our noticeboard.'

Sister Coulter looked at Jeni questioningly, before taking the paper and reading it. Jeni could have left her to read it on her own, but she decided to stay. If they had anything to say to one another, it was better for them to say it then and there, and then forget about the whole episode.

As Sister Coulter read, a flush darkened her cheeks. She did not raise her eyes for several moments after she had finished reading, but eventually she looked up and said, 'I suppose I owe you an apology.'

'Only if you wish.'

'Who *did* take the drugs?'

'That I'm not allowed to say,' Jeni told her.

'Oh, well!' Sister Coulter glanced at the clock on the wall. 'It's almost nine. If you get Mrs Brown's pre-med ready, I'll check it for you.'

She unpinned the drug cupboard keys from inside her pocket and held them out to Jeni. Jeni, realising

that was all the apology she was going to receive, took
the keys and made her way to the drug cupboard.

Word travelled fast in the hospital, as it always did,
and Jeni received a variety of responses to Matron's
bulletin. Almost everyone was happy for her, and all
were curious to know more. Jeni was glad she could
say, 'Matron has ordered. . .' As the day went on, she
gathered that the hospital grapevine was well and truly
frustrated for once. She hoped it remained so until the
question of who had taken the drugs died the death of
a nine-day wonder.

Halfway through the morning, Marc Adams
appeared. He was wearing a long dark green gown,
with a mask about his neck and a green cap pushed
back on his head. He had obviously slipped away from
OR between operations. It was also clear that he had
not come to see patients but to see Jeni, and that,
although he was genuinely pleased for her that it was
all over and she had covered herself with glory in the
process, he was nevertheless just a little disgruntled
that she had not confided the truth of the matter to
him.

'You must have thought me very foolish to go
rushing down to the beach to see you that day,' he
said.

'Not at all!' she protested. 'I really appreciated your
doing that. I wanted to tell you what was going on, but
Matron was quite adamant.'

'Medes and Persians, eh? But I do think you should
make some sort of restitution to me.' He looked at her
quizzically.

She raised enquiring eyebrows at him as, with a small
tremor of excitement, she wondered what that restitution might involve.

'What about dinner on Friday night? And some dancing, perhaps, this time?'

'I'm rostered for a late on Friday, but there might be someone who would change with me. Come into the duty-room while I check the book.'

He followed her into the room and waited as she took a black-covered book from a drawer.

She smiled as she saw who was rostered for early duty on Friday. 'I think I might just be able to work a switch,' she told him.

'Could that be a look of unholy glee on your face?' he asked.

She laughed. 'Machiavellian is the word! It's just that one of the sisters owes me one, and I doubt that she'll refuse when I ask her to change shifts with me.'

Marc had been laughing with her, but suddenly he became serious and, before she had a chance to take evasive action, he had cupped her face in his hands and kissed her on the lips. It was a firm kiss but not a lingering one. She did not have time to react or respond before he released her, said, 'I'll be in touch about Friday,' and was gone.

Jeni remained, very still, where he had left her. She could still feel the pressure of his lips on hers. She felt very much like a small child who had been given a sweet, only to have it snatched away after the first tantalising taste.

CHAPTER EIGHT

SISTER COULTER was in the treatment-room, seated at a bench, making computations on a sheet of paper. Jeni came straight to the point.

'I'm not in the habit of asking favours, but would you be willing to change times with me on Friday? I'm rostered late—I'd like to be early, if possible.'

Sister Coulter gave her a long look, then pursed her lips. 'I guess I owe you one. OK.'

'Thanks.'

'Heavy date Friday night?' Sister Coulter asked. Jeni read the question as being an attempt at friendliness, and answered evenly,

'A date—I wouldn't say a heavy one.'

'With Dr Adams, I presume?'

'As a matter of fact, yes. But how did you know?'

'I heard you had friends in high places. And I saw him go past a few minutes ago, in theatre gear, and he didn't seem to be worrying about patients.'

'It's no big deal,' Jeni told her. 'We happened to meet, for the first time, on the plane from England, a couple of weeks ago.'

Sister Coulter grunted, then looked down at the paper in front of her. 'Would you check my calculations on this drip rate? It's for Mrs Selby's Nitrostat.' She pushed the paper along the bench.

Jeni looked at the figures at the top of the page and asked, 'Microdrip tubing?'

'Yes.'

Jeni made some rapid jottings, then said, 'I make it nine drops a minute.'

'So did I. Thanks. And, incidentally, my name's Meg.'

End of hostilities! Jeni returned to her duties with a lighter heart on several counts.

When she got home that afternoon the phone was ringing. She dropped heavily into an easy-chair as she answered it.

'Hi, honey!'

'Tony!' she exclaimed. 'I should have rung you!'

'Oh? Why?'

'To tell you the drug business has all been cleared up.' Jeni recounted the story briefly. What she didn't tell Tony was that not once during the day had it occurred to her to ring and tell him about it. Once that would have been her first thought.

Tony was intrigued at the role she had played in bringing the culprit to justice. 'I'm glad it's all worked out well for you.' Then he said, 'Look, honey, we need to have a talk. . .soon. Could we meet somewhere?'

'Here?'

'No—we're still hectic at work. If we could make it some place near here I could snatch just an hour off duty.'

'I'm free on Thursday morning,' said Jeni. 'What about eleven o'clock in the Domain?'

'Fine! See you then.'

On Tuesday morning Jeni was again summoned to Matron's office. A mystery virus had depleted the staff in the operating unit. Matron had had reports of how well Jeni had done during the two emergencies on her ward last week. Would she be willing to relieve in OR for the time being?

In spite of the polite wording, it was a command rather than a request. Not that Jeni would have refused—she loved theatre work. But she hesitated before replying, and Matron noticed it.

'Is there a problem?' she queried.

'Only that I've made arrangements for Thursday morning and Friday night, based on the ward roster.'

'Leave that to me. I'll see that you're free for those periods. You may report to OR immediately, then.'

Thus it was that when Marc Adams, gowned and gloved and masked, walked out of the scrub-room an hour later and took his place beside the table, he was not at first able to place who was the nurse behind the mask who turned from her instrument table to greet him. Her eyes twinkled at him as she said, 'Good morning, Doctor.'

His eyebrows shot up. She could tell he was pleased as well as surprised to see her there, but he said only, 'Good morning! Sister Tremaine, is it not?' Jeni was glad, in view of the fact that the hospital seemed to be speculating about a possible relationship between them, that he was being circumspect.

But it was good to be working with him. And this time not only for a passing emergency, but for as long as it took the virus-afflicted staff members to recover. Jeni wished them well, but hoped they would not feel it incumbent on them to rush back to work too soon.

She had known instinctively that she and Marc would work well together. She realised very soon that he was an expert and most experienced surgeon, so much so that she wondered how long he would be satisfied to work in a small hospital like this and, indeed, how he had come to be here in the first place.

All at once, everything was going well for Jeni. Working so closely with Marc, seeing him practically

every day, she felt supremely confident that Liz just
wouldn't stand a chance. Just the fact that she and
Marc, right from the beginning, worked so well
together confirmed that. It must mean that there was
some basic compatibility that would help tremendously
when it came to building a relationship with him.

The first operation he did was the removal of a
Meckel's diverticulum. That was followed by a ligation
of a saphenous vein. Jeni did not have to scrub for
both procedures, but she elected to do so, and the
other nurses were happy to comply when she suggested
that it would be a good thing for her to get to know the
ropes as soon as possible, in case any emergencies
eventuated, when speed and familiarity with the unit
would be called for.

As Marc ligated the long saphenous vein and then
inserted a series of interrupted stitches, she became
engrossed in the deft, quick movements of his hands,
sometimes so near to her own as he accepted ligatures
and needle-holders from her. She wished the morning
did not have to come to an end.

When the skin sutures had been inserted and dressings and bandages applied, he stepped back from the
table, peeled off his cap and pulled down his mask.
Jeni could see that he looked more than just satisfied—
he looked happy. As happy as she herself felt. As she
caught his eye she couldn't resist smiling at him—let
the staff make what they liked of it. He saluted them
all gaily and went off, saying, 'See you all tomorrow.'
But it was Jeni he was looking at as he said it.

No, she was sure Liz didn't stand a chance.

On Thursday morning Jeni took a ferry from Manly to
the city. There was a light, pleasant breeze while they
were on the water, but she knew, as they turned left

into Circular Quay, almost under the huge span of the Bridge, that it was going to be very hot in the city. By the time she had walked up Macquarie Street and into the Domain she was thankful to sit down in the deep shade beneath the huge Moreton Bay fig tree where she had met Tony often in the past.

He arrived within minutes, flustered and apologising for being late.

'You're not really,' she said, and patted the grass beside her. He sat down, but seemed uneasy, unsure how to begin what he wanted to say. He picked a twig from the ground and twisted it between his fingers.

'The weather's a bit much, isn't it?' he said.

'I'm not complaining. After England it's a nice change.'

He said nothing, but turned and looked across at the Art Gallery where a group of school children were alighting from a bus. Jeni realised she was going to have to help him out.

'You want to split up, don't you, Tony?'

He turned, looking startled but relieved. 'How did you know?'

'It was fairly obvious, really. Nothing's been the same between us since I came back.'

He grunted agreement.

'What I don't know is why,' she said.

Tony scratched at a patch of bare earth with his twig, then said bluntly, 'It's Liz.'

Surprise kept Jeni silent for a moment. Then—'Liz? You and Liz?'

'Yes. I'm sorry. . .'

'Since when?'

'About a month after you left. We both landed at the flat one Friday night, planning to spend a quiet weekend there. Neither of us knew that the other had the same idea. It was odd,' he said reflectively, 'I'd never been alone with Liz before—not to really talk to her.'

'Was talking all you did?' It was a straight question, but Jeni felt she had a right to know.

'Well, no. . .well, yes, that weekend, anyway. Later on. . .well, you know. . . In fact, we met quite a few times at the flat. We both felt guilty about that, with you away. I hope you don't mind too much.'

'I would have been livid if I'd known at the time. Now—well. . .' Jeni shrugged and was silent, analysing her feelings. She did feel hurt—and humiliated, realising that all her friends had known what was going on and she had been so completely unsuspecting. But already all that was fading into insignificance against the realisation that, if Tony and Liz were involved with one another, she had nothing to fear as far as Marc and Liz were concerned. Everything else faded into insignificance beside that one fact.

She turned to him and said, 'I can honestly say I don't mind at all.'

With the declaration, her pride was restored. But even that didn't seem to matter against the thought that the last thing standing between her and Marc had been removed. Of course, Marc would be disappointed to learn about Liz and Tony. But he had known her for such a short time he could not have formed a lasting attachment to Liz.

Tony was looking surprised, relieved and a little aggrieved, all at the same time.

'I've been dreading telling you this, but obviously I needn't have lost any sleep over it,' he said.

'It's been fairly obvious that things weren't working out for us,' Jeni admitted. 'But I do think you might have told me before this. It would have explained why everybody has been so strange towards me since I came back—that really had me worried! I can see, now, they've been treading on eggshells, trying to keep your secret.'

'I'm sorry—that was my fault. I asked them not to say anything until I'd told you myself. Liz and I intended telling you that night we came to the flat, but Marc was there. And since then there hasn't been much opportunity.'

'So, now that I do know, I hope we can all be friends again?'

'Liz and I would like nothing better.'

It seemed strange to hear him say, 'Liz and I' like that. For so long it had been 'Tony and Jeni'. Now it would be Tony and Liz. She felt a pang of nostalgia for the old close friendship she had had with Tony.

He stood up. 'I must get back,' he said.

'Me too.'

He extended both his hands and helped her to her feet. They stood facing one another, still holding hands.

'I'll miss you,' he said.

Jeni burst out laughing at the look on his face. Like the small boy he was at heart, he wanted to have his cake and eat it too. She put her arms round him and he hugged her back.

'Be happy, Tony.'

'You too, honey.'

'I intend to be. Now, off you go to work.'

He grinned and began to walk away, but turned and waved, as if reluctant to finally close the book on that chapter of his life. Jeni waved back, stooped to pick up her bag and, with light steps and feeling like anything but a girl who has just been jilted, she made her way back to the Quay, and thence to the hospital.

The morning's surgical list had been completed when she arrived at work. Unless an emergency came in, staff duties would consist of cleaning, checking stock, paperwork. . .

Jeni was disappointed to think she would not see Marc. So, when she ran into him, literally, around a corner, just after five o'clock, he was greeted by a dazzling smile as he steadied them both by grasping her upper arms tightly. For an instant she thought he was about to draw her into a real embrace, but he dropped his hands and took a step back.

'You look as though life has been doing all the right things to you today,' he said, returning her smile.

'I couldn't have put it better myself,' she replied jauntily.

'I tried to ring you at your flat this morning, to make arrangements for tomorrow night.'

'I've been out most of the morning,' she explained. 'I met Tony in the city.'

'Oh.'

His smile vanished. Jeni realised he thought he had found the reason for the sparkle in her eyes. She didn't want to prolong their conversation, standing in the corridor as they were, but she had to say something, to avoid any more misunderstanding between them. There had been too much of that already.

Without preamble, she told him, 'Tony and I have broken up.'

'Oh? I'm sorry!' He looked at her keenly. 'Are you all right?'

'I'm fine.' She glanced around her. 'Marc, can we continue this tomorrow night?'

'Of course. I've made a reservation for eight. Shall I call for you at seven-thirty?'

'Please. I'm looking forward to it.'

The prospect of their date buoyed her up for the rest of the day. She was busy, but her duties were not demanding and she was able to give half her mind to planning what she would wear. She mentally reviewed each item in her wardrobe, but nothing seemed to meausre up to this very special occasion.

Finally she decided to throw discretion to the winds and buy something new. She would not have time to shop around, but a boutique in Neutral Bay had, more than once in the past, had just what she had needed. She would stop off there tomorrow, on her way home from work.

That evening, the phone rang.

'Hi, Jeni. It's Liz.'

'Hello, Liz. I was half expecting to hear from you.'

'Tony told me he saw you this morning.' Liz sounded hesitant, unsure of herself.

'Yes. I met him in the Domain.'

'He said you were really understanding. I wasn't sure whether that was just wishful thinking on his part. I'd like to think you aren't too upset, because I've been feeling pretty low about it all.'

'I knew the break had to come,' Jeni said. 'The only thing I've been sore about is that you didn't tell me sooner.'

'Could I come out and see you so we can talk properly?' asked Liz. 'We've been friends for so long. I hope we still can be.'

'Of course. And I'll be glad to see you. When can you come?'

'I was wondering about staying a couple of nights, if that's OK—tomorrow and Saturday?'

'I'll be out Friday night, for dinner,' said Jeni. 'I can catch up with you on Saturday.'

'With Marc?'

'As a matter of fact, yes. If *you* don't mind!'

'What do you mean?' Liz asked.

'I had the distinct impression on Saturday that Marc was more interested in you than anyone else.'

'I think you got the wrong idea,' laughed Liz. '*I* had the distinct impression he had me labelled as the wicked lady in the eternal triangle, and was doing his best to keep me away from Tony, for your benefit.'

'I don't follow you,' said Jeni, puzzled.

'I think he suspected, that night in the flat, that there was something going on between Tony and me, and he didn't want you to be hurt.'

'That's an interesting theory. I wonder. . .?'

It would be quite typical of Marc—thoughtful, kind, paternalistic. Jeni was not too sure she was thrilled about it, though. If Liz's surmise was correct, where did that leave Jeni in relation to Marc? Surely, if he cared for her at all, other than in a fatherly way, he wouldn't have tried to protect her relationship with Tony against the intrusion of a third party? Still, she supposed, it was better than nothing—she would just have to work all the harder to make him see her in a different light, starting with her date tomorrow night.

'Liz,' she said, 'if you're coming over tomorrow, how would you feel about meeting me at Peppers—you know, that boutique in Neutral Bay—after work? I've decided to splurge on something special for the night and I'd be glad of a second opinion.'

'You *are* going all-out! It sounds like fun. I shan't be able to be there until about four, so you make a start and I'll help with the final choice, if necessary.'

'Thanks. See you then.'

By the time Liz arrived at Peppers the next afternoon, Jeni had narrowed the choice to two outfits. One was an understated black silk dress with shoestring straps and a swathed bodice that sat just below the swell of her breasts. It was outrageously expensive, but even trying it on made her feel excited.

The other was just the opposite—a fine cotton in apricot tonings, with plenty of lace, a high neckline and tiny sleeves. With a full skirt and handkerchief hemline it was romantic and pretty.

Liz sneaked a look at the designer labels and whistled.

'You must like him a lot!' she whispered, so the sales lady could not hear. Jeni smiled, but said nothing.

In the end they decided on the black silk because, at the crucial moment of decision, Liz said, 'Accessories?' and Jeni realised she had just the things to set off the black dress—black taffeta shoes and a small black evening bag with an Art Deco diamanté clasp. She had bought the bag to console herself after a rare argument with Tony some months earlier. She wondered, fleetingly, whether she would ever have occasion to resort to such measures if her relationship with Marc developed.

As they left the boutique, Jeni carrying the precious dress, swathed in tissue paper in a big box with an impressive label, she said, 'Thanks, Liz. If you hadn't come, I probably would have set my finances back six months by walking out of the door with both of them.'

Liz looked thoughtful. 'So Marc is the reason you didn't mind breaking up with Tony?' she asked.

'Yes. But, even without Marc entering the picture, I think Tony and I would have recognised that we were never anything more than good friends. And I'm glad we did realise that, before we went any further.'

'I'm glad too,' said Liz.

CHAPTER NINE

HAVING Liz there, making comments and suggestions, was more fun than dressing for her date alone.

Liz prepared a snack for herself and Jeni had a quick cup of tea and a couple of cracker biscuits with pâté, before applying herself to her hair and make-up. Her hand was a little unsteady as she applied eyeliner and she had any number of nervous butterflies doing a dance inside her.

But when she slipped the black dress over her head, they all vanished. It looked so right! And it really was perfect with the gold of her hair and her light, glowing tan. Thanks to her bikini sunbathing, there were no pale spots revealed by the low neckline of the dress.

With Liz sitting on the bed, making approving noises, Jeni added a single strand of ivory pearls, then hesitated over the pearl-drop earrings which Tony had given her. Liz knew they had been a gift from Tony, but after all, they were all being very pragmatic about the switch in relationships. She looked at Liz enquiringly, and seeing her nod and grin, screwed them into place. They were just right—the perfect finishing touch.

Jeni had no reason to be disappointed with the look in Marc's eyes when she opened the door to him. He seemed almost stunned for a moment, a little smile playing about his mouth as he looked her up and down. His one word, 'Beautiful', wiped away for ever any concern that she had been too extravagant.

He was about to draw her into his arms there and

128

then, when he became aware of Liz, sitting at the table in the dining alcove, gazing out of the window and trying hard to look as if she were not there. Jeni drew him further into the room.

'Do we have time for some champagne with Liz before we go?' she asked.

'I've got a reservation at Butler's, at Potts Point, for eight o'clock. You'll know better than I how long it will take to get there,' he answered.

Jeni said, 'We have a few minutes,' and began pouring drinks.

Liz was impressed. 'Butler's, eh?'

'You know it?' Marc asked.

'I haven't been there for some time. It's lovely, and the food is excellent.'

Jeni asked, 'Bill's suggestion again?'

Marc laughed as he accepted his glass from her. 'No. This was too important an occasion to risk on one man's say-so. We had a round-table conference at lunchtime yesterday. It stirred up a lively discussion on eating places in Sydney, which was most interesting. Then one of the men suggested a place called William's, which they all recommended for after-dinner dancing. It's apparently rather exclusive, but he said all we need to do is mention his name, and we're in.'

'It sounds very exciting,' said Jeni, then asked, 'Do the men know who it is you're taking out dining and dancing?'

Marc looked apologetic. 'I wouldn't have told them without knowing first how you felt about it, but I'm afraid Bill let the cat out of the bag. I hope you don't mind. You'd forgive him if you heard how he described you to the other men!'

Jeni blushed faintly. 'I think I'd rather not know.'

They savoured their drinks and the view from the

balcony for a few minutes more. Liz did not take much part in the conversation, and Marc seemed restrained in her presence, not at all as he had been with her on the boat on Saturday. Jeni wondered whether he blamed Liz for her break-up with Tony. Well, it would not be long now before all those misunderstandings were ironed out. And then. . .

Marc handed Jeni into the car as though she were a piece of delicate Dresden china. He looked a little serious as he got behind the wheel. But then he turned to her, and what he saw in her face made him visibly relax. He smiled at her and said, 'You look very lovely tonight.'

Jeni replied, 'You don't look so bad yourself.' They both laughed, and with that the last suggestion of constraint between them vanished.

'Obviously the break-up with Tony hasn't depressed you too much,' he said.

Later on, she might tell him the reason she could look so happy, so soon after a broken relationship. All she said now was, 'I knew it was coming. I suppose I'm relieved that the break was clean and painless.'

'Does that mean you're still on good terms with Tony?'

'Oh, yes! I hope I always shall be. I guess I should have been wise enough, a long time ago, to recognise the difference between friendship and. . .love.' She spoke the word softly, shyly almost.

'And you're wiser now?'

'I think so.' She smiled up at him.

Marc took his eyes from the road for long enough to give her a searching look. He said nothing, but, as he turned his attention back to his driving, she felt the car slow down. Soon he flashed a left-turn signal and turned into a side street. It was a tree-lined avenue and definitely not on their way to Potts Point. Jeni was about to say, 'You've taken a wrong turning,' when he pulled into the kerb and stopped the car beneath a huge, leafy jacaranda tree. The glow of a street light came softly through the foliage.

She turned to him with a question on her lips, but he forestalled her by asking quietly, 'Is there any reason, *now*, why I shouldn't kiss you?'

She said, 'None whatever,' and lifted her face to his. Just before his lips met hers she closed her eyes and knew how much she had been waiting for this moment.

His kiss was not demanding, as it had been that first night, but long and lingering and wholly delightful. When at last his lips left hers, they wandered over her closed eyelids, then gently down the line of her jaw to the hollow in her throat.

It was the perfect moment that Jeni hoped would never end. But it was only the prelude to a perfect evening.

Marc was not only everything she had ever wished for in a romantic partner—he was a charming and attentive host and an entertaining companion. As they waited for their meal to be served and then ate it, they talked about anything and everything. It seemed he wanted to know every detail about Jeni's life, and she was happy to tell him. They discovered they liked the same movies, laughed at the same kind of jokes, had dreamed of travelling to the same exotic places. They abhorred, equally, stuffed shirts and arrogant medicos, were both at their worst early in the morning, their best late at night.

They forgot their food and held hands across the table in the restaurant. It was only afterwards that Jeni realised that, although they had discussed her past life exhaustively, he had said practically nothing about his.

Later, they walked, arm in arm, down the hill to William's. The night air was cool and refreshing, and Jeni felt full of life and eager to dance with Marc.

And dancing with him was all she had dreamed it would be.

With her head against his shoulder and his arms about her, she drifted to the music, in a state of blissful detachment from her surroundings.

'Enjoying yourself?' he asked once, teasingly.

She sighed. 'There's a cloud that's been specially designated for evenings like this,' she said.

Neither of them wanted to be reminded that Marc had surgery scheduled for early the next morning. When they finally drove back to Manly, they walked a little way along the beach, hand in hand, Jeni carrying her shoes. The warm night air was soft as a caress on her skin. It was two a.m. when they turned the key in the door of the flat and crept in for one last drink.

Marc asked for mineral water, and Jeni poured one for herself too. They carried their glasses through to the balcony and closed the door, talking in muted tones so as not to disturb Liz.

There were two steamer chairs, with cushions, on the balcony. They took one each. Marc was quiet for several minutes, sipping his drink thoughtfully. Then he turned to her with a smile and said, 'You're a long way away, over there.'

She stood up, took the cushion from her chair and dropped it on the floor beside him. She sank down on to it, and it took only a touch of his hand for her to lean back against his knee. His hand caressed her hair, as he said, 'There are things I should tell you, Jeni— things you need to know.'

His voice was serious and she knew, instinctively,

that she didn't want to hear, didn't want to know, whatever it was he felt he should tell her.

She must have made some small movement of objection, because he laid a hand on her shoulder, drawing her closer against him. Her moment of trepidation passed.

'You're right,' he said. 'Not tonight. But, with people coming and going here, and you on shift work and me so often on call, it seems impossible to find an opportunity to talk—and we must, soon.'

Jeni nodded. 'I know it seems a bit like Piccadilly Circus in the rush hour here, at times, especially in the summer. That's the worst of being so near the beach. Not that I mind, as a rule. And now that Tony and Liz are out in the open, there are likely to be even more comings and goings.'

'Tony and Liz?' he asked sharply.

'Yes. I haven't told you that that was why Tony wanted to break up—he and Liz started seeing each other while I was in London.'

'And you didn't mind, finding out about that?'

Jeni made a quick decision to tell him why she did not mind. Any reservation she had had about telling him had quite evaporated during the evening.

She said, 'You remember that day on the boat?'

'Of course.'

'You and Liz seemed to be getting along so well. I thought you were attracted to her.'

He looked at her keenly. 'So?'

She did not answer directly, but digressed.

'I sensed Tony wanted to break up, but I had no idea it was because he and Liz were involved with one another.'

'And it didn't bother you when you did find out the reason?'

'No.'

'Why not?'

He seemed to be pressing her, probing, almost as though he guessed her reason and wanted to hear her say it.

She said, very quietly but distinctly, 'Because, if Liz and Tony were together, it meant that she was unlikely to suddenly become involved with you.'

There, she had said it! Hardly daring to wonder what she might see there, she looked up into his face. He was shaking his head, as if in wonderment.

'And that made you happy?' he asked.

'That made me very happy.'

Taking her face between his hands, as he had that day on the ward, he kissed her. But this was no teasing, tantalising kiss. It seemed to Jeni that it was a seal, a promise, establishing a claim.

Then he said, 'It's even more imperative, now, that we talk. Could we have a couple of days away together, a weekend, somewhere quiet, as soon as we can both get the time off?'

She stood up, walked to the railing, and gazed out across the dark water, knowing that this was her moment of commitment. But she did not even have to weigh pros and cons. Her answer could only be one thing.

She turned towards him. 'Yes,' she said. 'Let's do that.'

Marc stood up and moved to join her, laying his hand over hers where it rested on the railing.

'How soon can you get days off?' he asked.

'I have next Friday and Saturday. Is that too soon?'

'No. I'll cancel my bookings for those days—or pass them over to my partners. That's the best of being in a large practice.'

Having made the decision, Jeni was eager, her mind busy with practicalities.

'Do you have any idea where we could go?' she asked.

'No. Do you mind looking after that?'

'North coast or south coast?' she mused. 'South coast would be cooler. But it might be hard to get anywhere, still being school holidays. I could go into the Tourist Bureau on Monday and see what's available—collect some brochures, and then we can decide together on the place.'

It was almost like planning a honeymoon. She had quite forgotten that the object of the exercise was for Marc to tell her things she was reluctant to hear. She was confident that any obstacles in their path would be insignificant, evanescent, not worth a second thought.

'Good!' He seemed as happy as she was at the prospect of their weekend. 'I really must go. Do you mind if I call you after surgery tomorrow? It won't be till mid-morning.'

'That's fine.'

She accompanied him to the door, where he kissed her again, lingeringly, and said, 'If it weren't for that surgery. . .! Who'd be a doctor!'

CHAPTER TEN

By the time Jeni returned to work on Monday, she was so used to being on cloud nine she felt as though it was her natural habitat.

Marc had rung, not once, but three times since Friday night. And now she had not been on duty for more than an hour than here he was, dressed in a scrub-suit, walking into the ante-room and greeting her with a special smile before donning his mask. The smile was still in his eyes as he ranged himself at a basin beside her and they both began to scrub for the first procedure on his list. It was an operation for the correction of a hammer toe, for which no assistant surgeon was necessary, so they were alone for the time being.

Above the sound of running water and the rhythmical swish-swish of their brushes, he said, 'I've been thinking. . .could I drive you into town after you finish work today, to collect some brochures from the Tourist Bureau?'

'Good idea. Then we could make our bookings on the spot.'

'I'll wait for you out front—at what time?'

'Three-thirty.'

They concentrated on their scrubbing again, until Jeni laughed softly behind her mask.

He turned his head to look at her, his eyebrows raised. Jeni said nothing, but glanced down at her brush and across at his. He chuckled too, as he realised that they were moving in perfect unison, up and down, up and down. . .

Perhaps, that too is a good omen, thought Jeni.

Soon after that the scout nurse came and waited, to tie their gowns after they had slipped into them. After she had gone again and they were pulling on their surgical gloves, Marc murmured, so that Jeni hardly heard, 'It's amazing!'

'What is?'

He looked startled, as though he had been talking to himself and did not expect a response. 'I can't believe it's only three weeks since we first met on the plane.'

She knew what he meant—that life had changed completely in those three weeks—and she had a sudden desire to reach out and make physical contact with him. But that was the last thing she could do at that moment. But as she preceded him into the theatre she knew that her life, right now, was just exactly as she wished it to be, and that the future held everything of which she could possibly have dreamed.

At the Tourist Bureau that afternoon, they talked with a cheerful, competent female assistant and came away with bookings made at a hotel in Bowral, in the Southern Highlands about three hours' drive south of Sydney. Even if the weather continued hot, the highlands would be cool. And there were lovely walks, a golf course, tennis, a pool.

'It's a shame we can't spare a week,' Marc said. 'Maybe later. . .'

On the drive back from the city, they made plans for their trip. 'If we leave in good time, we can browse through some of the towns on the way. Perhaps have a Devonshire tea somewhere,' said Jeni.

'Do you know how long it is since I had a Devonshire tea? It sounds marvellous.'

Everything was marvellous. Too marvellous to last.

As they approached Kirribilli, Marc asked, 'Would you mind if we dropped in to my unit? We have a practice meeting at the clinic at seven and I should pick up my mail and phone messages so that I'm up to date with what's going on.'

'Of course not,' smiled Jeni.

'You haven't seen where I live yet. Will you come upstairs with me?'

The unit was very much a male bastion. The large sitting-room majored in dark leather, polished wood and a collection of artefacts its owner had obviously collected on his travels.

While Marc flipped quickly through a pile of letters and opened two or three that looked important, Jeni sat down in the most comfortable chair she had ever experienced. When he had quickly scanned his letters, he pressed buttons on the recording machine beside the phone and listened to two brief messages, one from a professional colleague, one from a receptionist at the clinic. Then he uttered an exclamation of surprise as a woman's voice, very distinct, very British, began speaking.

'Marc—it's Greta. I'm sorry to have missed you. I've finalised things here earlier than I expected and managed to get flight bookings this week. We'll arrive in Sydney Friday morning, ten-thirty Australian time.' Then followed a flight number and something about 'how much we're looking forward to seeing you' before the voice was cut off in mid-sentence.

But Jeni had stopped listening. Friday morning. That was this coming Friday morning, when she and Marc were to have been on their way to Bowral. Yet this woman was confidently expecting him to be at the airport when she arrived from England. She sat waiting to hear what he would decide to do, but already seeing their weekend fade away like some impossible dream.

Marc stabbed a finger and stopped the machine.

'Damn!' he muttered.

Picking up an opened telegram from the table beside the phone, he read it and said, 'That's a week earlier than she said.'

Frowning, he sat down opposite Jeni and gave a loud sigh of frustration.

'Jeni, I'm so sorry. . .so disappointed. There's absolutely nothing I can do about this. I simply must be there to meet them.'

She nodded mutely, not trusting herself to speak. And what could she say, anyway? He was obviously as upset about this as she was. He walked across to her quickly, drew her up and put both his arms about her, straining her to him, as though defying fate, or anything else, to take her away from him.

'We'll do something. We'll manage somehow, even if it's only for Saturday. I'll say I'm tied up for the day. . .it won't be the same as a weekend, but it will be something. And maybe in a week or two, we can have our weekend.'

With his arms still about her, he drew back and looked down into her face.

'Are you OK?' he asked gently.

'I think I'd feel better if you would just. . .kiss me.'

With a muffled exclamation, his mouth descended on hers. When finally he released her, her knees were so weak she had to sink back into her chair. Flushed and breathless, she looked up at him and laughed.

'I don't think I can even remember what our problem was!'

He laughed with her, then looked at the clock on the wall. 'I'd almost forgotten that practice meeting. And

I must make a couple of phone calls first. I'll still have time to get you home.'

'I can take a ferry.'

'I won't hear of it. We'll make the most of what we have. And we'll make up for our lost weekend, I promise you.'

Jeni listened as he made his phone calls, one to the clinic and one to the hospital. As always, she admired the swift confidence with which he made decisions and the crisp clarity of his orders relating to his patients.

They did not talk much during the drive home but, whenever possible, he took his left hand from the wheel and held hers tightly, so tightly, once or twice, that she wondered just what was going through his mind. There was still so much she did not know about him.

When they were nearly home, she said, 'I'll phone and cancel the reservations first thing in the morning.'

Marc nodded. 'I was wondering whether you'd come to the airport with me on Friday morning. It would mean a lot to me.'

'If you want me to.'

'I do, very much,' he assured her.

It wasn't so much that she wanted to meet his. . .friends—in her mind, she had almost called them his 'family'—as that she wanted to salvage whatever she could of their lost weekend. There would be the drive to the airport, which would take an hour or more, depending on traffic. And yes, she admitted to herself, she was curious to see this Greta—even to observe the moment of meeting between her and Marc. Also, she could support Marc when it came to opting out of any suggestions Greta might have for including him in their activities on Saturday. She had a feeling Greta could turn out to be one strong-minded lady.

Certainly she would go with Marc to the airport.

Before then, there were three days to be got through. In those three days she found she had lost some of her confidence about the future. Not that there was anything in what Marc had said to have caused that. But it was there, nevertheless, that niggle of doubt.

To make matters worse, in spite of the care she and Marc had taken, the staff seemed to have got wind of something developing between herself and him. It was fairly inevitable that a new, young, handsome doctor should arouse interest and that any predilections he evinced would be the subject of speculation. Helen McMahon knew by now that he was not married, after all, and on Tuesday afternoon, when there was nothing much happening in OR she appeared on a somewhat flimsy errand, manoeuvred to get Jeni alone and then asked, 'How was your date?'

Jeni replied, 'It was fine, thanks,' and changed the subject firmly enough to discourage any further questions.

Meg Coulter, too, asked Jeni about Friday night, one day when they had run into one another in the dining-room. Meg was the kind of person who could have been envious of Jeni's friendship with Marc, and Jeni had noticed that she did not wear any rings. But one of the nurses in OR told Jeni that Meg had been 'living with a guy for several years' and though gossip had it that they 'had their ups and downs' Meg apparently was not looking to make a change, so her question about Jeni's date was probably quite disinterested.

Jeni was rostered for late duty most of that week and saw very little of Marc, but she gathered, on the one or two occasions she did meet up with him briefly, that he was very busy in the absence of one of his partners.

But, he assured her, he would be free on Friday, and also on Saturday.

He called for her quite early on Friday morning. He kissed her and complimented her on her appearance. She was wearing a crisp, loose white cotton top and caramel-coloured, cuffed, knee-length shorts, with Italian sandals—a smartly casual outfit, and cool.

Marc seemed subdued, and as the dense traffic demanded all his attention until they were over the Bridge and through the city, Jeni said very little too. Then she suggested that it might be a good idea if he filled her in about Greta and the children.

He nodded and obliged. 'Greta's the widow of Paul, a cousin of mine. He and I were close—closer almost than brothers. You see, my parents were killed in a car smash when I was seven.' Jeni made a sympathetic sound, but he went on, 'I was an only child and Paul's parents adopted me. Paul was three years older than I and there were two older sisters.'

He manoeuvred his way through a busy intersection, then continued.

'Paul took me under his wing, young as he was, and I hero-worshipped him. I guess that was why I chose medicine as a career—whatever he did was good enough for me. He became a very successful consultant physician, with a large practice in London.'

Jeni, realising that Marc was not yet familiar with the route to the airport, interrupted him, to suggest that he move into the right-hand lane, ready to make a turn. He did so, then went on with his story.

'Paul married young, but I didn't follow suit in that. He could afford to, I couldn't. My parents had left a certain amount, enough to get me through med. school and buy into a practice, but that was about all. My uncle wanted to treat me the same as he did Paul, and

he could have afforded it. But I had an independent
streak, as far as money went, and I'd already taken so
much from him.'

'And Greta was Paul's wife?' Jeni prompted.

'Yes.'

By the tone of his voice, Jeni realised she would not
hear a lot more about Greta unless she persisted, and
she very much wanted to know about her.

'How long has she been a widow?' she asked.

'Paul died of a rare form of Hodgkin's disease three
years ago. Sarah was seven then and Kim four. The
kids have adjusted pretty well, as kids do. But Greta's
found it very difficult, even now. She's still restless and
unsettled, and. . .'

He did not finish the sentence. Jeni, turning her head
slightly, saw that his face was closed and remote. She
knew he did not want to continue the conversation, but
she had to know more.

'And you feel you have a responsibility to Greta and
the children?' she pressed.

'Yes. For Paul's sake, and also for his parents'. It
was difficult for them all, following Paul's death. But
his mother's dead now, and his father's living with the
older daughter and he's very wrapped up in her family.
There are two little girls whom he dotes on, to the
exclusion of his other grandchildren. That's a part of
growing old, I guess. And Greta never got on well with
her in-laws.'

Sensing his reluctance to say more, Jeni left it at
that, although she still had unanswered questions. Why
had Marc come to Australia? Remembering his reaction when she had asked him that in the restaurant on
their first night out, she could not bring herself to ask
it again.

And why were Greta and the children following him

to Australia? By now he must have fulfilled any responsibility he had to them. Clearly, money was not a part of their problem.

And how long did Greta plan to stay in Australia? For some time, obviously, or she would not be bothering about schools for the children.

Jeni sighed. She guessed she would find out what she wanted to know in good time.

The airport was crowded and Marc had to park some distance from the terminal. By the time they reached the arrival lounge, the plane from England had landed and its passengers were already trickling into the lounge from Customs and being swallowed up in the waiting throng.

It was not long before Marc, standing tall and scanning the crowd, said, 'There they are!' and began pushing eagerly through the crush of people. Jeni followed more slowly and stopped some way short of the group to whom he was holding out his hands. She was in time to see him embrace a woman who looked vaguely familiar and whom she could now recall having seen at Heathrow. The embrace lasted a little longer than Jeni would have expected, and their kiss seemed to her to be more ardent than was usual between friends. She reminded herself that they were *old* friends who had shared deep experiences, such as the loss of a man who had been husband to one and close friend to the other.

Nevertheless, the sight of that meeting increased her reluctance to intrude into the group. She wondered whether she had been wise to come at all.

Marc released the woman and turned to the children, affording Jeni her first real opportunity to study Greta. What she saw did not reassure her.

Greta was tall—not as tall as Marc, but probably

above five feet eight inches. She carried her blonde head proudly and looked, to Jeni, the complete aristocrat. Her hair-style, swept back from the face into curls at the back, accentuated the beautiful bone structure of her face. Her eyes were green, her skin pure and creamy.

She was wearing a superbly cut lightweight cream skirt and an emerald-green silk blouse which brought out the green of her eyes. A small smile—a complacent smile, it seemed to Jeni—played about her lips as she watched Marc and the children.

Jeni turned her attention to the children and was immediately enchanted by the girl, who was talking animatedly to Marc. She had a small, elfin face which was alight with joy as she talked. Her hair was a dark auburn and she had arched eyebrows which added to her elfin look. Jeni could not see the colour of her eyes, but she too had a peaches and cream complexion. The Australian sun would play havoc with that, if they were not careful!

Kim was as fair as his mother, which revealed that Greta's colouring was her own. He was more solidly built than Sarah. He was standing, watching Marc and Sarah, with his head slightly bent, blue eyes looking up from beneath a thatch of straight hair. Jeni sensed he was bewildered, not really understanding what was happening to his small world, but prepared to face it head-on. He responded with few words when Marc turned to draw him into the conversation.

As Marc straightened up from talking with the children, Greta, perhaps aware of Jeni's continued scrutiny, turned her head and her eyes met Jeni's. Jeni smiled tentatively. At once Marc moved to her side and, with a hand beneath her elbow, drew her into the group.

'I'd like you to meet a friend of mine,' he said. 'Jeni, this is Greta. And Sarah. And Kim.'

Jeni smiled and said, 'Hello,' to Greta and, 'Hi,' to each of the children. She asked about their flight and they exchanged the remarks usual at times like that.

It was not long before Marc said, 'Let's get out of this crush. Greta, I assume this is yours?' indicating a trolley laden with very expensive-looking pieces of luggage.

'Yes. The rest is coming freight, in a few days, I hope.'

'Right. Don't get lost, you two,' to the children. 'Jeni, would you keep an eye on them? This crowd seems to be getting worse.'

They made their way to an entrance door and stopped just inside. The noise was less here and they were able to talk more comfortably.

'We had to park quite a way away, Greta,' Marc explained. 'I think I should get the car while you stay here with the luggage. I'll have to come out of the car park and then come round and pick you up. It'll take a few minutes.'

'Can we come with you?' asked Sarah eagerly, agog to see what this strange new land they had come to was like. Running to meet whatever experiences it had to offer, thought Jeni.

Kim was more specific. 'Will there be any kanga-roos?' he asked.

'Not here,' Marc explained seriously. 'But it won't be long before we come across some. Perhaps not today, though.' Then, to Greta, he said, 'What do you think? May they come?'

'Yes—if you don't mind taking them.'

'Then we'll probably be about ten minutes.'

He walked off, with a child at either hand.

Jeni looked around. 'There's a vacant seat over there. Why don't we push the luggage over and sit down while we wait?'

They were no sooner seated than Greta asked bluntly, 'Where did you meet Marc?'

Jeni explained about their encounter on the plane, and added, 'It's hard to believe that was only a few weeks ago. So much has happened since.'

As soon as she had said it, she realised how Greta might interpret it. Sure enough, Greta looked at her sharply, enquiringly. Jeni hurried on, explaining how surprised she and Marc had been to find they were working at the same hospital, and trying to imply that they were no more than professional acquaintances.

But Greta appeared sceptical about that.

'Marc told me that a sister from the hospital helped him find a school for the children. Was that you?'

'Yes, it was,' said Jeni, and was not at all surprised when Greta did not express gratitude for her assistance. Indeed, Greta was looking less and less pleased. She said, 'I'll need to see the schools myself before making the final decision. But I was told we should enrol them as soon as possible for the new year intake.'

'That's right. He was fortunate to find a school that could take them.'

'It would have been better if we could have come out with Marc,' Greta went on, 'but I still had business matters to finalise.'

She paused for a moment, then said, as though she was just making conversation, or telling Jeni something she expected she already knew, 'We're going to be married, you know.'

The bottom dropped out of Jeni's world.

For a moment that seemed to go on for ever, she couldn't breathe, couldn't think. She must surely have misunderstood what Greta had said. When she could, she asked, in a voice which she hoped sounded reasonably normal, though very much aware that Greta had not missed a small part of her reaction, 'Married? Who? You and. . .'

'Marc and I, of course.'

Jeni turned her head, as if expecting Marc to reappear through the entrance door and awake her out of this nightmare. As her world stopped spinning and she became capable of something like coherent thought, she realised that she had been subconsciously steeling herself against some such revelation. Marc had seemed so reluctant to talk about Greta. Now she knew why. But she had not expected anything quite so definite, and certainly not so soon.

'Didn't Marc tell you?' Greta pressed home her advantage.

'No. After all, it's none of my business.'

'There are probably other things he hasn't told you. Do you know why he left England?'

'No.'

The single syllable was as much as Jeni could manage. It expressed the tide of negative feeling that threatened to engulf her. What she really wanted to say was, 'I don't want to know. Don't tell me.' But she could not manage that.

'He was charged with making improper advances to a patient.'

'No!' Jeni exclaimed again, and this time it was an emphatic statement of rejection and disbelief. To allow no possible risk of being misunderstood, she added vehemently, 'I don't believe it!'

But, even as she said it, she recalled Marc's reaction, that night in the restaurant at the Rocks, when she had asked him why he had come to Australia. And then how he had looked when she had told Patti that female patients often fell in love with their doctor.

But that was no proof that he was guilty. She simply would not believe that. She could not understand why Greta, who said she was going to marry Marc and therefore, presumably, must love him, should tell her such a thing.

She said, 'He may have been charged with something like that, but I'll stake my life on it he wasn't guilty.'

She saw something flicker in Greta's eyes, and knew that, by the very vehemence of her defence of Marc, she had revealed her feeling for him. Greta would know now, for sure, that she and Marc were more than just casual acquaintances.

She stood up, grasped the handles of the luggage trolley, and began to move towards the entrance. As she did so, Marc walked quickly through the door. He looked at her and saw in her face the shock, the anger, the bitter disappointment she did not have time to wipe from it, even had she wanted to. He looked beyond her to Greta and his face whitened. He closed his eyes for a second, as though trying to wipe from his mind what he had seen. Then, with a rigid face and tight lips, he grasped the handles of the trolley, turned his back and walked away.

Greta and Jeni followed, saying nothing, ignoring one another, like the strangers they were.

Marc stowed the luggage in the boot, then held the doors for Jeni and Greta to get into the car, Greta in the front, as though it were her right, Jeni in the back with the children.

Marc too had become a stranger.

CHAPTER ELEVEN

THE DRIVE back from the airport seemed interminably long. Jeni wanted nothing more than to run away and hide, away from Marc, away from Greta, away from the shattered ruins of her dreams for the future.

Marc's reaction, when he saw the shock in her face, had confirmed Greta's statement that he was going to marry her. Jeni knew, with a sick certainty, that that was what he had been going to tell her on the weekend that she had looked forward to so happily. She had been naïve, gullible. Marc had told her there was something she should know, but she had had her head in the clouds and hadn't wanted to be told.

She sat behind Greta, looking at the back of her head, and came as near as she ever had to hating anyone. Not because Greta was going to marry Marc, but because of the vindictiveness she had displayed in taking the very first opportunity of telling Jeni so, and in attempting to discredit Marc in Jeni's eyes by revealing facts about his past which he naturally wanted very much to forget. She had seen in Jeni a rival for Marc's love and had tried to drive a wedge between them.

How could Marc love anyone so lacking in even the smallest drop of the milk of human kindness?

Greta was chattering away, trying to appear relaxed, pretending there was nothing amiss. Marc was answering Greta in monosyllables, and although Jeni could not see his face, she knew it still had that drawn, shocked expression.

Sarah and Kim had become very quiet, sensing the tension between the adults. Sarah, wide-eyed and alert, was looking from one to another, trying to understand what was going on. Kim sat well back in his seat, no less aware of the strained atmosphere, but dealing with it in his own way, by retreating into himself.

Indignation for the children came to Jeni's aid. They were too little, too vulnerable, to be expected to cope with this as well as the major changes that had already taken place in their small world. She turned to them with a warm smile and said lightly, 'Well! You haven't seen much of Australia yet, but do you think it's going to be much different from England?'

'It's very hot,' said Sarah. 'There was snow at home.' Her bottom lip trembled and Jeni squeezed her arm comfortingly.

'We have snow, too, in winter. Not in Sydney, but not too far away. You must ask your mother. . .and Marc. . .to take you to see it later on.'

Marc sensed what she was doing and made an effort to follow her example. He said, with forced lightness, 'Sarah and Kim have always called me Uncle Marc. What do you think, kids? Shall we make it just Marc?'

The children made uncertain sounds, not sure whether their mother would think that the right thing, or whether they would feel comfortable about doing it. It would certainly be appropriate, thought Jeni. They could hardly go on calling him Uncle after he and Greta were married.

Marc continued, 'There'll be lots of exciting things to do. Jeni's friend has a boat. Perhaps he'll take you out on the water some day.'

Greta turned her head and looked at Jeni with sudden interest.

'Is your friend a doctor?' she asked.

'Yes.'

Greta could make what she liked of that. Jeni had not the slightest intention of enlightening her about her personal life.

Greta, undeterred, asked, 'Does he work at the same hospital?'

Jeni said, 'No,' repressively, and turned to talk with the children. Greta did seem more natural after that—less brittle and artificial.

Kim was losing his withdrawn look and responding to Jeni's advances. Soon there was lively conversation in the back of the car, with little bursts of laughter from Sarah. Jeni tried to block out the murmur of voices from the front seat. Even had she wanted to know what they were talking about, she could not have done so because they kept their voices low.

Suddenly Jeni felt that the car was a prison and she had to escape from it as soon as possible. They were approaching the city when she said quickly, 'Marc, I have things to do in the city. I'd like you to drop me off, please.'

His head jerked up and she could feel his eyes on her in the rear-view mirror. He knew that she had nothing planned for that day and was manufacturing an excuse to get away. She kept her gaze on the passing parklands, refusing to look at him.

He tried to discourage her. 'It'll be very hot in town. Why don't you come back and have lunch with us at my place?'

His use of the word 'us' hardened Jeni's resolution.

'It'll be cool in the stores. I have some things to drop off for Tony, so I may have a snack with him.'

He knew, as well as she did herself, that she had not the slightest intention of seeing Tony. She knew nothing of Tony's movements these days.

'You'll still have to get home in the heat,' he persisted.

'I'll catch a ferry. It will be lovely on the Harbour.'

He nodded unhappily, accepting that there was nothing he could say to persuade her to change her mind.

Greta turned and looked over her shoulder at Jeni.

'Are you working tomorrow, Jeni?'

There was no warmth in her voice, but the hostility had gone. She seemed to have accepted that Jeni did not, after all, constitute a major threat to her future with Marc.

Jeni said flatly, 'Several of my friends will be spending the day at my unit, which is near the beach. We'll be swimming, surfing, maybe have lunch on the beach.'

That was all true, except that it would be 'they' and not 'we' who would be doing that. She had expected to spend the day with Marc, as he had promised. Now the day was a blank. She would have to find somewhere to go, away from everyone.

'I wonder whether Sarah and Kim could join in your picnic? They'd love a day at the beach. Then Marc and I could start house-hunting. We can't stay in a hotel indefinitely. I'd like to get settled down in our own home as soon as possible.'

The sheer effrontery of the woman took Jeni's breath away. Even Marc made a protesting sound. Now was the time for him to make the excuses he had promised Jeni he would make, to tell Greta that he was not free tomorrow, that he had other plans. But he did not do so, and Jeni, knowing, now, that he would have used the day to 'talk' to her, and what it was he would have told her, was thankful to be spared that much.

Sarah and Kim had pricked up their ears at the mention of a beach picnic. Jeni, having no intention whatever of spending the day making merry with her friends, felt trapped and resentful. If Marc had any understanding of how she was feeling, surely he could do something to extricate her from her dilemma, and suggest something else that would appeal to the children? But he said nothing, and she knew she could not disappoint them. Anyway, she thought, what have I to lose? We needn't go to the picnic, but I can take the children off somewhere. It will keep them happy and occupy my time and thoughts. While Marc and Greta. . .

Angrily rejecting that line of thought, she turned to Sarah and Kim, who were eagerly awaiting her decision.

'All right, I'll be very happy to spend the day with you two.' She was rewarded by their joyful smiles. 'But I don't think a beach picnic in this weather would be wise—you'd be as red as lobsters after half an hour in our sun. I'll think of something else and we can do the beach another day, when it's not so hot.'

'What time should we start tomorrow, Marc?' Greta asked.

She was almost cordial now. And why shouldn't she be, thought Jeni, with everything going her way?

'Whenever you like,' Marc replied mechanically.

Jeni turned to Sarah and Kim. 'I'll talk to you guys later, then, and make a time, huh?' Then she added coldly, 'You can drop me here, Marc.'

But when she sat, a little later, in the remotest corner of a dimly lit coffee lounge in George Street, it was not plans for the following day that occupied her mind.

She went back over and over again, each time she had met Marc, every conversation they had had. She soon saw, in the light of Greta's statement that she was going to marry Marc, that it was not what he had said that was significant, but what he had not said.

There had been no word of commitment, no promise of an ongoing relationship, no talk about the future. He had kissed her ardently—she felt herself flush at the memory of his kisses and her reponse. But he had never once said, 'I love you'. He had said her name, 'Jeni,' in a tone that made it an endearment, but he had never called her 'my darling', or any of those other words which came so readily to the tongue of a person in love.

Jeni had been vaguely aware of these omissions, but she had been too happy to stop and consider what they meant. She had been too much in love to be analytical. But now it was all clear, fitting together like a jigsaw puzzle of which Greta's revelation had been the key piece.

And that weekend in Bowral? Did he think that she would have been willing to stay there with him, once she knew about Greta? Would he have told her at the beginning, or waited until the two days were almost over? He would have told her gently—oh, so gently, because that was his way. Perhaps he would have pointed out that he had made no commitment to herself. Would he have expected her to say she didn't mind and put a good face on it? Spend the remainder of the time with him, drive back to Sydney together?

She shivered suddenly, grateful, after all, that the weekend had never taken place, that she had found out in time.

Her cup of cappuccino was almost cold. She drank it at a draught, paid her bill and made her way down to Circular Quay. There she let a hydrofoil go and waited for a ferry. The ferry was not crowded at that hour, and she sat outside where a breeze of the ferry's making made the heat a little more bearable. Just being on the water was soothing and she was able, after a time, to get her mind off the treadmill of futile questions which had no answer.

The last time she had been on the ferry was when she had met Tony in the Domain and had come away so happy because now she was free, and Marc was free, and the future seemed golden. A sudden yearning for the old, uncomplicated relationship with Tony possessed her. It might have been only friendship, but friendship, after all, had a lot going for it. Love, romance, infatuation—whatever it had been, it hurt too much.

The door of her flat swung open almost before she had inserted her key in the lock. James stood there, looking as surprised to see her as she was to see him. She knew there would be folk coming and going on these two days, but she had not expected James to be one of them.

But if she had to see anyone just then, she was glad it was James. He was so unobtrusive, although he was not unobservant, and somehow Jeni didn't mind when she saw that he knew, immediately, that all was not well with her world.

He did not rush right in and ask what was wrong, but said, 'I hope you don't mind my being here. My folks are away this weekend and I gathered it was sort of open house here.'

'Of course I don't mind. I'm glad to see you.'

And she was. It was better than coming home to an empty flat, or, worse, to one filled with a noisy, merrymaking crowd.

'I've just made a sandwich. Have you eaten?' he asked.

'I've had coffee, but that's all. A sandwich sounds great. I'll fix it—if there's anything in the fridge. I left it rather bare this morning, thinking everyone would be bringing their own rations.'

'The girls gave me a long list this morning and I've been shopping for hours,' James told her. 'I'm not exactly Speedy Gonzales in a supermarket, but the larder's now replete.'

Jeni put together a salad sandwich, helped herself to a can of somebody's Coke, and joined James in the living-room.

'So you're hitting the beach with everyone else tomorrow, are you?' she asked, knowing that, although he enjoyed sailing, he was not renowned for his prowess on a surfboard.

'I guess so, but you know what I'm like in anything more than a two-inch swell,' he laughed.

An idea began to take shape in Jeni's mind. She decided to see how James felt about it.

'Weather permitting, how would you feel about doing something rather different tomorrow?' she asked him.

He looked curious. 'Such as?'

'Such as accompanying me and two children to Australia's Wonderland.'

'That *would* be different! But I thought you were off somewhere with Marc tomorrow?'

'Change of plan.' She could not keep a tremor out of her voice and she looked away to hide the tears that burned behind her eyelids and tightened her throat.

James did not press her, but asked, 'Who are the kids?'

'Sarah and Kim, aged ten and seven. They arrived with their mother from England this morning. Greta is some sort of connection by marriage to Marc. He and I met them at the airport.'

Again James accepted the bare bones of an explanation, although he looked as though he was trying to read between the lines.

At that moment the phone rang, jangling harshly at Jeni's elbow. She jumped, reached out a hand to pick it up, then drew back. What if it was Marc? She looked pleadingly at James and said, 'Would you?' then moved away to the other side of the room.

James picked up the receiver, said, 'Hello. Oh, it's you, Marc,' and raised his eyebrows at Jeni, who shook her head violently.

'No,' he said, 'I'm afraid she's not here. Can I take a message? OK. Be seeing you.'

'No message. He'll ring later,' he told Jeni.

She nodded wordlessly. James looked at her for a moment, then moved across and sat beside her on the settee, taking her hand in his.

'Do you want to talk about it?' he asked, with a wealth of understanding and sympathy in his voice. It was almost too much for her composure. She turned towards him and buried her head in his shoulder.

'Thanks. Not yet. Perhaps later,' she said in a muffled voice.

He put one arm round her and, with his free hand, stroked her hair. She remained there for a moment, then sat up, feeling rather embarrassed by this unusual situation between herself and James, and moved a little way away from him on the settee.

He asked, in an everyday tone, 'Why do you have to have the children tomorrow?'

'Because Marc and Greta will be house-hunting. Greta asked me to have Sarah and Kim, and I could hardly refuse.'

'I see,' said James, looking as though he wished he had someone there for a few minutes, to tell him, or her, a thing or two. 'I'll be happy to come along tomorrow. It'll be a first for me too.'

'Thanks again.' She put out a hand and touched his cheek fleetingly.

He made a slight movement, but checked and looked at his watch, saying, 'The mob will start arriving soon. Some of them are bringing sleeping bags. It sounds like a good recipe for insomnia to me! Anyway, it's not my scene. How about having a hamburger with me somewhere and seeing a movie?'

'You don't know how much I'd like that! Just give me five minutes.'

Remembering James's culinary predilection, Jeni suggested they eat at a Lebanese restaurant not far away. To be fair to him, she made an effort to throw off her gloom and they had a friendly, very enjoyable meal. But the movie was a different matter. In the darkness, when it was no longer necessary to make an effort to look and sound cheerful, her despondency returned. By the time they left the cinema she could not have said what the film had been about.

As they came out, a cool wind was blowing and cars were swishing along a wet road.

'That's better,' said James. Then, 'How keen are you to go back to the flat?'

'Not at all. I'd be a spectre at the feast tonight.'

'My mother keeps an ever-ready spare room. It's yours for the night, if you want it.'

'You seem to have all the right answers tonight,' smiled Jeni. 'But I'd need to be back to meet the children in the morning. Unless I make a quick sortie to the flat now, and pick up everything I'll need for tomorrow.'

'And leave from my place in the morning. Good idea.'

It was done. James stayed in the car while Jeni went up to the flat. She donned a bright smile before entering, said, 'Hi, everybody! I'm just passing through,' vanished into her bedroom and reappeared five minutes later with a small overnight bag. In reply to a chorus of voices, she said, 'I can't stop now,' and was almost out of the door again when Liz caught up with her.

Closing the door behind them, Liz said in a low voice, 'Marc's rung for you twice. I took the calls and didn't tell the others who it was. He sounded pretty agitated. I thought you were with him. What's happened?'

She looked worried—concerned for her friend. Liz had begun nursing training on the same day as Jeni and they had been through many ups and downs together. Jeni felt she owed her an explanation now.

'I met Marc's English friends with him at Mascot this morning. Apparently, so Greta told me as soon as she had an opportunity, she and Marc are going to be married.'

Liz gasped. 'No!'

''Fraid so!' shrugged Jeni.

'And Marc hadn't said anything to you about it?'

'Not a word.'

'What a heel! I'm sorry—really sorry! You must be feeling utterly wretched.'

'That, and more!'

'But if you aren't with Marc, where are you going now?'

'I dragged James off to a movie. He's offered me a bed at his parents' place. I didn't feel I could face the crowd here,' Jeni explained.

'Of course not. Will you and James be back for the picnic tomorrow?'

'No. I'm looking after Greta's children while she and Marc go house-hunting.'

'You're kidding! He asked you to do that?'

'It was Greta's idea. And it seems that, where Greta leads, Marc follows.' Jeni sounded bitter, even to her own ears.

'I think that's. . .unspeakable!'

'Oh, they're nice kids. James and I plan to take them to Wonderland, now that the cool change has come.'

'Good old James. He's a treasure.'

'I'm beginning to realise that,' said Jeni.

'You could do worse, you know.'

'Liz—don't!'

'Sorry.'

'That's OK. Have a good day tomorrow. You won't tell anyone about Marc and me? Let them think I'm with him.'

'Right.'

In the small, dainty spare room in James's parents' home, Jeni slept reasonably well, after making a determined effort not to think about her troubles. She woke to the ringing of the phone and, as James had said he was going jogging early, she got out of bed, made her way groggily to the sitting-room and picked up the receiver, confident that it would not be Marc because he did not know where she was.

It *was* Marc.

He must have expected that her instinct would be to hang up immediately she heard his voice, because he said, without greeting or preamble, 'I must talk to you.'

'Isn't it a little late for that?' she queried.

'I hope not. I know I should have told you earlier

about. . .everything. But you seemed so happy—we were both so happy. I didn't want to spoil that.'

'Yes, I was happy. I never thought. . .'

Angry with herself for allowing him to hear the break in her voice, Jeni went on firmly, 'I can't see any point in discussing things now. We can't take back the past—what's done is done. Let's leave it at that.'

'If that's how you want it. But I'm extremely disappointed.' Marc was not pleading now. Instead, his voice was angry and cold. But what reason had he to be angry and disappointed? Unless it was disappointment that he had not been able to entice her away for that weekend, before Greta arrived and put the record straight.

In level tones, she said, 'James intended ringing you this morning, to ask you to bring the children here, instead of to the flat.'

'I suppose I have no right to ask you what you're doing at James's home.'

'No, you haven't.'

'It didn't take you long to find someone to console you,' he said bitterly.

'That's despicable!' she flashed back at him. 'You know very well my flat's being used by everyone this weekend, since I'd expected to be away.'

He said nothing, and the silence on the line stretched out interminably. Jeni was about to hang up, when he said, 'Are you still prepared to have the children today? If you want to opt out. . .'

'You can't really believe I'd do that and disappoint them! James and I have an outing planned for them. If you'll bring them here by nine o'clock, we'll get them back to your unit by five.'

She gave him James's address. He said, 'Very well.' And that was that. No pleasantries. No 'Have a nice day.' Just another silence and then the buzz of the dial tone after he had hung up.

No sooner had Jeni replaced her receiver than the phone rang again.

It was Liz, and she was agitated.

'Jeni! Was that Marc you were talking to?' Without waiting for a reply, she hurried on, 'I tried to get in first to warn you, but your line was engaged. I had to tell him where you were. I had no choice—he threatened to come here if I didn't. He didn't believe you weren't here—thought you just wouldn't speak to him.'

'Don't worry, Liz. I can't avoid him for ever. James was going to ring him soon, in any case,' Jeni told her.

'Oh, good! I felt really grim about telling him. Are you still taking the kids to Wonderland?'

'Yes. And I intend to enjoy myself too.'

'Attagirl!'

But Jeni's sang-froid was not quite equal to answering the door when Marc arrived with Sarah and Kim. James met them and, after Marc had introduced the children to him, he stood his ground, giving Marc no opportunity to enter or to prolong his visit.

When the children heard that they were going to the biggest fun park in Australia, they could not wait to be on their way. James's car was a Mazda, and it instantly took Kim's fancy. When James invited him to sit up front he was in the seventh heaven. 'We'll put the girls in the back,' James announced, and Kim's enthusiastic nod showed that he too thought the back seat was the proper place for female mortals.

It was soon obvious that James had acquired a follower, and Kim a hero. James, who could be so remote at times, came down to Kim's level, and Jeni could not have said which of the two of them most enjoyed all the fun of the fair.

Jeni and Sarah were happy together too. It was the children's day, and James and Jeni gave them their head, trailing around behind them, placing no restrictions on their activities, occasionally joining them for a ride or a sideshow. It took some coaxing to drag Kim away from the huge roller-coaster which he was sure must be the 'biggest in the whole world.'

James got his hamburger today. They all did. And Coke, and ice-cream and bags of crisps and anything else that took their fancy. Jeni warned James that he would be sick tomorrow, as well as the children, but they all agreed it was worth it.

Jeni and James handed over two tired but happy children to Marc and Greta a little after five o'clock.

Jeni had said she would wait in the car while James took Sarah and Kim up to Marc's unit, but she couldn't resist Sarah's imploring, 'Do come too, Jeni!'

Neither James nor Jeni asked how the house-hunting had gone, and Marc and Greta did not volunteer any information. Even had they wanted to talk, they would have found it almost impossible to get a word into the children's excited account of their day.

Jeni felt the day had been worth the effort when Kim said, in a voice which was very like Marc's, 'Really, you know, Mother, I think Australia will be quite a good place to live.'

CHAPTER TWELVE

JENI went to work on Sunday morning with her resignation in her handbag. She knew that Matron was rarely in the hospital on a Sunday, but was dismayed to discover, from one of the girls in the change-room, that, because of the Bicentennial Australia Day holiday on Tuesday, Matron was taking a break right through until Wednesday.

Since the affair of the drugs, Jeni had built up quite a rapport with Matron and did not want to hand her resignation to anyone else. It was frustrating. The sooner she severed her connection with the hospital, the sooner she would stop seeing Marc. She contemplated asking to be relieved of OR duty and returned to the wards. But that too would have to wait until Matron returned. She would just have to make sure she avoided him as much as possible. Perhaps if she faked a cold she would not have to scrub for operations. She didn't know how she could endure working with him, standing as near to him as that entailed.

Fortunately, some of the surgeons were taking advantage of the long weekend too, and there was no surgery booked for today and very little for Monday and Tuesday. Consulting the bookings, Jeni saw that Marc's name beside one of the operations had been crossed out and somebody else's inserted. The handwriting of the insertion was Marc's. So he must be as eager as she was to avoid a meeting. It was absurd of her to feel so disappointed!

In the meantime, the staff had to be ready for any

emergencies that eventuated and make use of the spare time by doing a thorough check of the unit's instruments, equipment and stock, noting any that were in need of repair or replacement. They had to augment stocks of linen, gowns, dressings and drapes, check drug supplies, sutures and lotions, test batteries and electrical equipment. With a little effort, Jeni thought, she could become absorbed in the tasks to the exclusion of other thoughts.

There were two nurses, Paula and Carol, on with her. Jeni had the contents of the suture cupboard spread out on a table and was polishing its shelves when she heard the phone in the office ring. Paula was at lunch and Carol went to answer it. She came back to report that an emergency appendix had been admitted to the wards, was being prepped for surgery and would be up in an hour. That presented no problem. They could be set up and ready in less time than that. Jeni began to replace the contents in the suture cupboard. Then a thought occurred to her.

'Who's the surgeon?' she asked.

'Dr Adams.'

Jeni's heart plummeted. She was the only trained nurse on duty, so she would have to scrub. As she took sterile packs from cupboards and laid them on tables, she was resolving, first, not to allow her personal feelings to intrude on her work but to be cool and professional, and second, to minimise by whatever means she could the time she spent in Marc's presence.

To that end, she hurried through setting up the theatre and began to scrub earlier than she needed to, so she could be out of the scrub-room before Marc walked into it.

So the patient was on the table and Jeni, in full theatre garb, was doing a sponge check with Carol when Marc walked in, ready to begin operating. He spoke to the anaesthetist at the head of the table then, with his hands in the air, shoulder-height, said, 'Good morning, Sisters.' There was something in his voice that told Jeni he had already recognised her, even though her back was towards him.

She said coolly, 'Good morning, Doctor,' at the same moment Carol did, but when, for a fleeting moment, their eyes met, she saw in his a depth of unhappiness which, for all her anger and bitterness towards him, wrenched at her heart. There was just that momentary spark of awareness between them before the anaesthetist said, 'He's all yours, Marc.'

Marc held out his hand, saying, 'Lotion, please,' peremptorily.

Jeni felt herself flush. He knew very well he did not have to ask for whatever it was he wanted—not when she was working with him. She gave him a bowl of skin-cleansing lotion in one hand and slapped sponge-holding forceps into the other one. She also managed to catch his eye and was pleased to see his gaze falter before her direct, cold stare.

That was the prelude to an uncomfortable half-hour. His work was as precise and sure as usual. But he swore when he encountered an obstinate bleeding vessel. He appeared not to hear a remark the anaesthetist directed at him and it had to be repeated. He snapped, 'Denis Browne's,' when Jeni handed him plain dissecting forceps which were what he had used at that stage the last time she had done an appendicectomy with him.

And, to cap it all, he nicked a glove while he was using a heavy taper needle to suture the muscle layer. That meant he had to discard those gloves and don a fresh, sterile pair. And that meant that Jeni, being scrubbed, had to hold the new ones as he inserted his hands into them. The changeover did not take long, but they were, perforce, so close that their hands almost touched. Jeni, acutely aware of his physical closeness, shrank back almost imperceptibly. He was aware of it immediately and turned away abruptly, almost before he had his hand in the second glove. She was immensely relieved to be able to put the width of the table between them again and concentrate on the closing stages of the operation.

When the counting of sponges, swabs, instruments and needles was completed and the skin sutured, he did have the grace to say, 'Thank you, Sisters' almost apologetically. But then he bluntly refused Carol's offer of coffee, and it was no time at all before Jeni heard the door of the surgeons' change-room slam shut and quick footsteps fade away down the corridor.

Carol and Paula returned from taking the patient to Recovery as Jeni was beginning to clear away the clutter in theatre. Carol looked at Jeni and gave a low whistle.

'What was eating *him*?' she asked, almost as though she expected that Jeni could give her an answer. Fortunately she didn't wait for one, but went on, 'He's never behaved like that before. Perhaps we interrupted his game of golf.'

'Possibly,' said Jeni, and had to admit to herself that she didn't even know whether he played golf. Once again she realised how little Marc had ever told her about himself. Now she knew why—and the knowledge didn't make for happiness.

She did know, though, that his behaviour during the time he had been in OR had nothing to do with golf and everything to do with her presence.

Fortunately Carol had worked in operating-rooms

for long enough to have learned to be philosophical about the behaviour of surgeons, which was, at best, unpredictable, so she did not belabour the subject, and the three girls set about restoring OR to its usual state of preparedness for whatever might happen next.

Jeni was rostered for late duty next day. When she reported on she found there had been a run of minor emergencies and a hernia repair during the morning. But, apart from a suturing job on a foot, which, fortunately, did not belong to a patient of Marc's, nothing else came in that day and they were able to press on with their routine chores.

With so little happening, it seemed a long eight hours. Through the windows overlooking the Harbour Jeni could glimpse an unusual amount of movement on the water. Excitement was beginning to mount on the eve of Australia Day. She was thankful she would be on duty tomorrow and so able to avoid the celebration and jollification.

But Tony rang late that night, after she arrived home, and his enthusiasm was infectious. Those who had to work in the morning were making up a party to take out on the boat, after they had knocked off. He hoped they would be able to get in near Farm Cove, to see the First Fleet Re-enactment vessels at anchor, and to see the parade of tall ships down the Harbour from mid-afternoon. Then they would have a picnic tea on board—everyone bringing their own—and manoeuvre as close as they could for the fireworks display which was to be the climax of the day, at nine o'clock.

Jeni was reluctant at first. Then, realising she should make an effort to throw off the cloak of depression she had been clutching to herself, she said yes, she would go.

As she thought of fireworks, she remembered Sarah

and Kim. She had no idea what plans Marc and Greta had for the day, but to see the fireworks from the boat would be a special treat for the children. So, before Tony rang off, she asked, 'Would there be room on the boat for the children too?'

'Children? Which children? Have you been holding out on me?'

'Marc's children.' It slipped out and she realised that, in her thinking, she had been grouping them all together, Marc and Greta, and Sarah and Kim. If they weren't his children yet, they soon would be. But she wouldn't tell Tony that. 'I mean, Greta's children,' she corrected. 'She's some sort of distant cousin of Marc's by marriage and she's recently arrived from England.'

'Oh, yes, I remember now. Marc has been a sort of father-protector to them since their father died. He told me something of that situation on the picnic the other week. Sure, bring them along. I'll try and rustle up a couple of kid-sized life-jackets for them.'

'Thanks, Tony. You're a sport,' Jeni told him.

'Then we'll see you at the marina as soon as we can get there after work.'

He was in high spirits. Lucky Tony! Lucky Liz! Jeni gave herself a mental shake, looked at her watch and decided that, late though it was, she should ring Marc now, if there was to be any chance of the children coming with them on the boat tomorrow.

She dialled his number. Greta answered.

Jeni almost hung up without speaking, but realised, in the nick of time, that that would give Greta the satisfaction of knowing that her tactics to alienate her and Marc had been successful. So she said brightly, 'Jeni here, Greta.'

'Oh! Hello, Jeni.' Greta sounded affable, but curious.

'I'm sorry to ring so late, but I've just got home from the hospital. It didn't occur to me, when I saw Marc yesterday, to find out what plans you and he have for the holiday tomorrow.'

'You saw Marc yesterday?' There was an edge to Greta's voice now.

'Yes. Didn't he say? Anyway, what I'm calling about. Several of us are going out on the boat tomorrow, from about mid-afternoon. We'll see the tall ships leave, have tea on board and watch the fireworks. It occurred to me that the children would enjoy coming with us.'

'I see.'

'Is Marc there?' Jeni felt safe asking that, being fairly sure, from the conversation with Greta so far, that he was not in the unit.

'No, he's not. As a matter of fact, he's next door, inviting his neighbours to watch the celebrations tomorrow from our balcony. They don't have a view of the Harbour from their unit. Marc's invited some other people too.'

'Sounds fun. What do you think about Sarah and Kim?' Jeni did not want to prolong the conversation, in case Marc should return.

'I'm sure they'd like to go with you on the boat. Thanks for asking them. Shall we take them somewhere to meet you?'

'Yes—to the marina. Marc knows where that is. About three-thirty.'

'All right. Shall I send tea with them?' There was no mistaking, now, the hostility in Greta's voice.

'No, I'll make some extra sandwiches. Goodnight, then.'

'Goodnight.'

Jeni hung up, feeling wickedly satisfied that she had

given Greta something to think about, if she happened to be lying awake that night.

Jeni herself had one or two things to think about. What was Greta doing in Marc's unit at that hour of the night? And where were Sarah and Kim?

She had to remind herself, firmly, that Marc and Greta's domestic arrangements were no concern of hers. The sooner she accepted that, the better.

CHAPTER THIRTEEN

EVEN Jeni's low spirits were not proof against the excitement next day, as Australia celebrated its Bicentenary.

She was delayed, driving to work, by thick traffic, all heading towards the city and the Harbour, and she arrived at the Spit Bridge just as it was beginning to open. Not too concerned about being late today, she wound down her window to enjoy the cool morning air, and watched the unprecedented scene below. Yachts and motor boats, small craft of every description, were all moving in one direction, down Middle Harbour. It reminded Jeni of movies she had seen of the boats setting out to evacuate Dunkirk, though the objective of this armada today was so very different. There could hardly be a boat left in any marina further up, and the congestion on Sydney Harbour must already be awesome.

Detouring through Women's Surgical to speak to Helen on her way to OR, she found that the holiday atmosphere prevailed here too. Walking patients were settling into chairs on balconies which overlooked the water, planning to spend the day and part of the night there. Nurses were moving beds to give occupants the best possible view. Television sets were on in every room.

Thanks to the wide panorama from the windows of its ante-rooms, OR had a steady stream of visitors that day—staff from other parts of the hospital which lacked a view. Several doctors, scheduled to cover their

173

practices in the clinic, wandered across, considering
OR their special domain and knowing that there they
were safe from encounters with their hospital patients.
The coffee machine worked overtime and the biscuit
tin needed replenishing by mid-morning.

Not content with the view from the windows, Carol
made a sortie into the wards and returned trium-
phantly, with a porter in tow carrying a television set
she had 'borrowed' from a vacant room. So, as well as
their grandstand view, they could hear the commen-
tators, the speeches and the music, and see the pagean-
try and the dignitaries, of whom the Prince and Princess
of Wales were the stars, with the Princess in heritage
green and the Prince sporting a yellow tie and, later,
looking very much at home in an Akubra hat.

It was a thrilling and, at times, emotional day,
although, with two million people crowded on to the
Harbour foreshores and so many boats on the water
that, as one commentator said, 'You could walk from
shore to shore without ever touching water', it was
vastly different from the scene which would have
greeted the First Fleet vessels on their arrival two
hundred years ago. For one thing, the *Bounty*, two
hundred years ago, would not have been sporting a
huge advertisement for Coca-Cola on its topsail!

Jeni was standing to one side of a group watching
the television coverage of an Aboriginal protest march,
when a voice behind her said quietly, 'Hello, Jeni.'

She turned slowly, wishing he had not come today,
reluctant to be reminded of things she had almost been
able to forget amidst all the razzmatazz.

'Hello, Marc,' she said, in a flat, emotionless voice,
then she turned again to watch the screen.

'It's tragic, isn't it?' he said, after a moment.

Startled, she looked up at him, then realised that he too was watching the protestors on the screen.

'Some problems just don't have easy answers,' she replied.

'No. What's done is done, and there's no going back.' His voice was low, controlled and, Jeni thought, infinitely weary.

Of course, he was talking about the angry dark faces on the screen, calling for land rights and attention to their suffering. But she knew he was also talking about himself, and she could not follow his train of thought. What was there, in his past, or in Greta's, that made him look and sound so devoid of hope, as though it was transportation and exile he was anticipating, and not marriage to a beautiful woman whom, presumably, he loved?

Perhaps that was it. Did he love her? Or was he marrying Greta out of some stubborn English compulsion to do the right thing by his cousin who had once meant so much to him, but who was now dead?

Suddenly she knew she had to find out the truth.

They had drawn a little way back from the group around the television set, and she had no fear that their low-voiced conversation would be overheard above its noise.

'Why are you doing it, Marc?' she asked.

He looked at her, his brows drawn together, trying to fathom what she meant.

'Why am I doing what?'

'Marrying Greta.'

'*What!*'

The word was an explosion. Two or three people turned their heads and looked at him curiously, but immediately became absorbed again in what was happening on the television screen.

He was looking at her with riveted intensity, and, deep down in his eyes, she thought she saw something come to life. He grasped her by the arm, so tightly it hurt, and said, 'Where can we talk? I know. Come on!'

Unceremoniously he ushered her before him, out of the ante-room, along a short corridor, and into a room which at one end was the surgeons' change-room and, at the other, their lounge. It was most unlikely that anyone else would come here today, but, just in case, he closed the door and turned the key in the lock.

'Now, say that again!'

Bewildered by his reaction to her question, Jeni repeated it, tremblingly.

'Why are you marrying Greta?'

'Who said I was marrying Greta?'

Hardly daring to speculate where this conversation was going to end, but, unable to quench a sudden surge of hope, she replied, 'Greta certainly seems to be under that impression.'

He seemed to be struggling to control himself, biting back words he wanted to utter.

'When did she tell you that?'

'At the airport, that morning.'

She could not mistake the dawning of hope in *his* face too, now. But it was still suppressed, as though he was afraid to jump to conclusions in case they were the wrong ones.

'Did she tell you anything else that morning?' he demanded urgently.

Jeni concentrated, trying to recall what else Greta had said. The shock and the disappointment of hearing about Greta's expectations of marrying Marc had almost wiped away every other recollection. Then she remembered.

'She mentioned something that happened before you left England—something to do with a patient.'

'Yes? What exactly did she say?'

'I can't recall her exact words, but it was to the effect that you'd been charged with making improper advances to a female patient.'

'And what did *you* say to that?'

'At first I said I didn't believe her. But then I thought she'd hardly make up a story like that. And I remembered one or two things you'd said to me, that I hadn't understood at the time, but they made me think that possibly it was true. Anyway, it's just the kind of thing that can happen to a doctor.'

'You said that to her?'

'Something of the kind. I know I said that, even if you had been charged with such a thing, I was quite sure you weren't guilty.'

The tension drained from his face and his voice was not quite steady, as he said, 'Bless you, little Jeni!'

Her eyes brimmed with sudden tears.

'You surely didn't think that I'd believe you could. . .?' she began.

'What else was I to think? You were looking so stunned, so shocked, when I came back with the children. I was sure Greta must have told you the story, and that you'd believed it.'

Jeni shook her head slowly and said, quietly but with firm emphasis, 'No.'

How could he ever have thought that of her? That was why he had been so angry, so distant and hostile, these last few days. She moved towards him in an instinctive attempt to reassure him, to make him believe. . . Then she was in his arms and they were folded tightly about her. It was like coming home. It was where she belonged. It was so right and natural for her to be there, cradled against him, hearing the steady thump, thump of his heart beneath her ear.

When finally she slowly drew away, she said, 'I didn't know it was that. I couldn't understand why you were. . .like you have been.' She brushed a hand across his forehead, as if to smooth away the effects of those last few days.

'I've nearly been out of my mind,' he admitted. 'I was angry with Greta for telling you—angry with you for believing her. I told myself I'd trusted you, believed in you, when you were under suspicion about the drugs. And then, when the crunch came, you didn't believe in me. The way you looked at me when I came back into the Arrivals lounge. . .'

'I was in a state of shock from hearing that the man I was. . .' Jeni paused. '. . .that you were going to marry Greta. To be honest, I just didn't think very much about the other thing.'

'We might have gone on misunderstanding. We might never have known. Oh, Jeni!' He held her close again.

Then he drew back from her, took her hand and led her to a settee against the wall. He sat down beside her.

'I want to explain about what happened in London, then we can forget about it for ever.'

'That's not necessary,' she told him. 'We can forget it, without you going through it all again.'

'Let me tell you—I'd feel happier.'

She nodded. It might do him good to get it off his chest once and for all.

Marc began, matter-of-factly, 'I'd been seeing this woman, professionally, for some time, with what she said was right upper abdominal pain. She was convinced she had a gall bladder problem that needed surgery. She almost had me convinced too, for a while, but I ran a complete series of tests and excluded that and every other possible reason for her symptoms. I tried to get her to attend a pain clinic, but she refused, saying she had every confidence in me. That should have made me suspicious.'

He paused, remembering, then went on.

'I made the mistake, just once, of examining her without my nurse being in the room. It was a routine examination, but, later, it was my word against hers that absolutely nothing happened.'

Jeni nodded sympathetically, knowing how easily such situations could arise in a doctor's life. She recalled his face, that day on the boat, when they had all been discussing the ticklish situations that patients had landed each and every one of them in. Marc should have known that she would understand.

'Later on,' he continued, 'I became suspicious about her motives, and told her that I was discharging her from my care on the grounds that I couldn't do anything more for her. Then she became amorous—threw herself all over me. . .' He shuddered. 'I knew then how neurotic she was and how cleverly she'd disguised that, to me and, apparently, to other doctors as well. As it turned out, she was not only neurotic but vicious. "Hell hath no fury. . ." and all that. Even when I heard that she was laying charges, I thought it would be just a formality. But she was young enough, and attractive enough, for the court to think it was quite on the cards that I could have fallen for her. As I said, there was no evidence one way or the other. It was my word against hers. And she put on a very good performance in court.'

'How awful! But it was eventually resolved?'

'Yes. But not before it became very nasty and

attracted a lot of publicity. If I hadn't had such a good solicitor, goodness knows what would have happened. He ferreted out some facts that had remained well hidden, about her past medical history—her psychiatric history, in fact. I didn't know he'd done that, and if I had I wouldn't have let him use them in court—unethical and all that. But he said it was the life work of a dedicated doctor against protecting a neurotic woman who'd be all the better for a good public slap on the bottom.'

'I heartily agree,' Jeni said, then prompted, 'And so?'

'His revelations did what he hoped they would—she broke down in court—put on a real exhibition and virtually convicted herself in the end.'

'So that was that,' said Jeni.

'That's what I thought—naïvely. I thought I could just go back to work and forget about it. But it didn't go away. It kept cropping up. Then Bill came over from Australia for a few weeks and heard all about it, and suggested I come here—even offered me a chance to buy into his practice. I couldn't accept quickly enough.'

'And you were still smarting when I met you on the plane?'

'It showed, did it?' he said ruefully.

'I could tell you weren't happy.'

'Well, it's all behind me now. And if I hadn't come to Australia I wouldn't have met you, and that would *really* have been a tragedy.'

He kissed her again, and it was many minutes before Jeni sat up, gave a deep, blissful sigh and picked up her cap from where it had fallen on the floor.

'All this. . .and I'm on duty! I don't even know what the time is! Do you think anyone has missed us?'

Marc laughed and reached for her hand. 'I'm sure they haven't. Not today. Work is the last thing on anyone's mind.'

Jeni was suddenly serious.

'Were you ever in love with Greta?'

'No!' His denial was emphatic. He hesitated, then stood up and moved across the room to the window, looking down into the street below. The hum of traffic was muted by distance.

'We mustn't have any more misunderstandings. I know Greta has always hoped we would marry. There was one occasion. . .' He turned and faced her. 'Just one. I felt sorry for her and she was so persistent. I made it quite clear next morning that it hadn't meant anything and that it wouldn't happen again.'

He turned away, as if not wanting to see the subdued look on Jeni's face.

'When she said she wanted to come to Australia too, I told her again that although we could continue to be friends and I'd still watch out for the children, that was all she could expect from me.'

He thrust both hands deep into his pockets and his face was serious.

'Last night we really had it out, and I'm sure she's under no illusions now.'

Jeni was interested. 'What time was that?'

'It was after your phone call. She said you'd rung and why. She didn't say much else about that, but I could tell she was upset. Then she got emotional and it all sort of blew up, and I realised she'd still hoped things would work out and that was why she'd come to Australia, in spite of all I'd said earlier. But I had no idea—none whatever—that she'd said anything to you about marrying me. If I had. . .'

His face and his tone were grim. Jeni said hurriedly, 'What will she do now? Will she stay in Australia?'

'I think so. She wasn't happy at home—never did get along with Paul's family. I think it will be good for her and the children to make a new beginning. And she's bound to marry again—she's a very attractive woman. But definitely not my type,' he added hurriedly, seeing Jeni's raised eyebrows.

He came across the room to where she was sitting, held out his hands and drew her to her feet. At that moment there was the sound of hurrying footsteps in the corridor outside the room. Jeni straightened her hair and began pinning on her cap.

'Either it's lunchtime or there's a case coming up. In which case, someone might just want to use this room. You realise my name would be mud if I were caught locked in the surgeons' change-room with a doctor?' she said.

'What would they think if you were caught locked in a surgeon's arms? Because I seem to have caught some mysterious complaint. Unless I kiss you every few minutes I suffer from a severe form of deprivation.'

She laughed. 'It must be catching! I have the same symptoms.'

'Then there's only one thing to do.'

'Let me take my cap off this time, or it'll be completely ruined.' She giggled. 'I've just realised that I'm still wearing this——' indicating the shapeless white gown which almost reached to her ankles and was tied around the middle, which all OR staff donned as soon as they arived on duty.

'You look beautiful to me,' he said, and sounded quite as though he meant it. 'And that delightful fragrance I catch a whiff of every now and then—is it Eau de Betadine or Parfum de Meth?'

'Any more of that and *I'll* nick your gloves in theatre next time!'

He became serious. 'Wasn't that appalling? I haven't done that since my student days.'

'Carol told me you weren't your usual self that day, that you're usually such a nice, easy-going guy!'

'Me? Never! She just hasn't seen the real me.'

'I hope she never does.' Jeni's laugh became a gasp as his arms tightened about her.

They managed to leave the doctors' lounge a little later, without being seen. In the empty corridor, Marc kissed her on the tip of her nose and said, 'How soon can I see you?'

She considered. 'I must take the children on the boat for the fireworks tonight. I can't disappoint them.'

'Could I gatecrash? Would there be room?'

'Tony'll probably have the boat loaded to the gunwales. But come and we'll see. There's always the dinghy! We could tow you along behind.'

'As long as you were in the dinghy too, and I could be captain, I wouldn't mind at all,' he assured her.

Neither of them saw Carol poke her head around the corner to see what the laughter was about, then withdraw it with a surprised look on her face.

CHAPTER FOURTEEN

JENI arrived back at the flat that afternoon, feeling she was a different person from the one who had left it nine hours earlier. As she made sandwiches and packed fruit and biscuits into a picnic basket, she pondered the ups and downs of her relationship with Marc. Its highs had been so very high, its lows so very low. The one thing that had remained constant had been her feeling for him—her love for him, she admitted to herself. He still had not said that he loved her, but how could she doubt that, after this morning?

She sang as she showered quickly and slipped into a pair of jeans and a deep pink loose shirt. She gathered up some rugs and a bulky white pullover, in case the night should turn cool, and then Marc was knocking on the door, flanked by Sarah and Kim, who were fairly dancing with excitement.

The children chattered incessantly all the way to the marina, but Jeni and Marc were happy to listen and exchange an occasional smile and just be together. They walked from the car hand in hand, towards the group busy loading food and gear into *Rheya*, which Tony had obviously just brought alongside.

Liz's look of surprise when she saw them changed to one of delight when Jeni gave her a tiny nod. Tony too was grinning broadly as he said, 'Glad you could make it, mate,' to Marc. James was not there, but Jeni resolved to ring him, when she could, and tell him her good news and thank him for. . .just being James.

As Jeni had predicted, the boat was perilously low

in the water, but they were using the motor and not sail, and moving very slowly, especially once they joined the seething spectator fleet on the Harbour proper. The tall ships were already making their way down the Harbour, and it was a sight to touch the heart of the toughest landlubber.

Sarah's eyes were wide with wonder at the spectacle. Kim appeared no less rapt, but Jeni suspected that there was no boat on the water but *Rheya* as far as he was concerned, and that he was in some secret adventureland all his own.

As the last of the tall ships moved slowly past, they ate their picnic, making it last as long as possible so that the children would not become impatient, waiting for the fireworks to start. When it began to get dark, Jeni made them wrap themselves in the rugs she had brought and sit well down out of the breeze, which was becoming cool.

Tony, after working furiously all afternoon to avoid other boats in the worst maritime traffic jam Sydney Harbour had ever seen, had pulled *Rheya* into the lee of Shark Island, a little way off from the main crush near the Bridge. As the fireworks were to be fired off two barges, one near the Opera House and one further down the Harbour in the direction of Bradley's Head, they would have a perfect view of both.

Jeni and Marc sat in the stern of *Rheya* as she rocked gently beneath them. An occasional snatch of song came across the darkening water, from other boats, waiting like them, nearby.

Marc's arm was about her, holding her close. Against the background hum of conversation, nobody else could have heard his quiet declaration, 'I love you, Jeni.'

It was the first time he had said it, and it seemed to Jeni entirely appropriate that, at that instant, the first of the fireworks soared heavenward and the sky exploded with light and sound.

She said, 'I love you too,' but he could not possibly have heard her above the noise. In a momentary lull, she tried again, and caught his words, 'I've loved you ever since. . .' before he had to give up, laughing, and they sat watching the biggest pyrotechnic display Australia had ever staged, convinced it was just for them.

Eventually it was over. It took a long time to get back to the marina and longer still to drive home through roads jammed with traffic. Marc had to concentrate on driving and Jeni sat beside him, tired and happy.

Sarah and Kim were asleep in the back seat before Marc finally pulled in to the kerb outside Jeni's flat. He came around and helped Jeni out, closing the door softly. Then he took her hand in his and led her across the road on to the lawns that fronted the beach. There he stopped in the shadow of a tall pine tree and took her in his arms. After a few moments she murmured against his shoulder, 'Since when?'

He didn't have to ask her what she meant. 'Since I put you on the plane at Singapore, thinking I'd never see you again. I almost cancelled my stopover then and there.' He smiled down at her. 'What would you have said if I'd reappeared before the plane took off?'

'I'd have been glad. I was feeling I'd lost a friend. Perhaps, even then, more than a friend. I think my fate was sealed when you held my hand on the plane,' Jeni smiled.

He murmured something unintelligible, but his meaning was clear. Then he drew her back further into the shade to avoid being caught in the headlights of an approaching car. The car slowed down and stopped in front of Jeni's flat and several people got out, chattering, and disappeared inside.

'Your ubiquitous friends!' sighed Marc. 'Don't they ever go anywhere else? When we're married, my darling, we'll find ourselves a secluded house with a big iron gate and a padlock. And, to make doubly sure, we'll hang a huge DO NOT DISTURB sign on the front door—for the first few weeks, at least.'

But Jeni had stopped listening. She stood in a daze of happiness until his voice ceased. Then, raising her face to his, her eyes luminous in the moonlight, she asked, 'Have I just been proposed to?'

He looked surprised, then apologetic.

'I've been remiss. . . I guess I just assumed. . . But what else did you think today has all been about?'

She twinkled at him. 'A weekend in Bowral, perhaps?'

Marc took both her hands in his before he said, very seriously, very tenderly, 'Jeni Tremaine, will you be my lawful wedded wife, to be loved and cherished all the days of your life?'

'Yes!' she breathed. 'Oh, yes!'

The children slept on. Cars passed along the road. The moon cast a pathway of silver across the water. Tiny waves rippled in and broke softly on the sand. . .

— MEDICAL ❤ ROMANCE —

The books for your enjoyment this month are:

GIVE ME TOMORROW Sarah Franklin
SPECIALIST IN LOVE Sharon Wirdnam
LOVE AND DR ADAMS Judith Hunte
THE CHALLENGE OF DR BLAKE Lilian Darcy

♥ ♥ ♥ ♥ ♥

Treats in store!

Watch next month for the following absorbing stories:

GOODBYE TO YESTERDAY Sarah Franklin
CALLING NURSE HILLIER Elizabeth Petty
LUCY'S CHALLENGE Hazel Fisher
NO LEASE ON LOVE Jean Evans

Discover the thrill of 4 Exciting
Medical Romances — FREE

BOOKS FOR YOU

In the exciting world of modern
medicine, the emotions of true love
have an added drama. Now you can
experience four of these
unforgettable romantic tales of passion
and heartbreak FREE — and look forward to
a regular supply of Mills & Boon
Medical Romances delivered direct to your door!

❧ ❧ ❧

Turn the page for details of 2 extra
free gifts, and how to apply.

An Irresistible Offer from Mills & Boon

Here's an offer from Mills & Boon to become a regular reader of Medical Romances. To welcome you, we'd like you to have four books, a cuddly teddy and a special MYSTERY GIFT, all absolutely free and without obligation.

Then, every month you could look forward to receiving 4 more **brand new** Medical Romances for £1.45 each, delivered direct to your door, post and packing free. Plus our newsletter featuring author news, competitions, special offers, and lots more.

This invitation comes with no strings attached. You can cancel or suspend your subscription at any time, and still keep your free books and gifts.

Its so easy. Send no money now. Simply fill in the coupon below and post it at once to -

Mills & Boon Reader Service, FREEPOST, PO Box 236, Croydon, Surrey CR9 9EL

NO STAMP REQUIRED

YES! Please rush me my 4 Free Medical Romances and 2 Free Gifts! Please also reserve me a Reader Service Subscription. If I decide to subscribe, I can look forward to receiving 4 brand new Medical Romances every month for just £5.80, delivered direct to my door. Post and packing is free, and there's a free Mills & Boon Newsletter. If I choose not to subscribe I shall write to you within 10 days - I can keep the books and gifts whatever I decide. I can cancel or suspend my subscription at any time. I am over 18.

EP03D

Name (Mr/Mrs/Ms) _____

Address _____

_____

_____ Postcode _____

Signature_____

mps MAILING PREFERENCE SERVICE